Back To Win

How Johnny Moss Returned Humanity

to Poker and Life

Written by Ed Chiaramonte

Written by Ed Chiaramonte, 2020

Edited by Adam Lee

First Printing 2020 / Not For Sale

Published For Sale 2021

Copyright Pending

Cover picture of Johnny Moss reprinted with permission by

Special Collections and Archives, University of Nevada,

Las Vegas. Thank you Stacey for your help!

Cover picture of keyboard credited to Raymangold22 and

Wikimedia Commons @

https://commons.wikimedia.org/w/index.php?curid=374103

91.

Cover artwork created by author.

"Do you know," he said, "if one of them fellows was to make a book about my life, it would be a real book, a crackerjack, not one of them made-up books, y'unnerstand, not one of them fancy books you read and don't believe... Y'know, if somebody was to make a book about my life, all the hotels along the Strip would take it on. They'd display it everywhere 'cause they all know I'm a respectable gamblin' man... It'd sell too. 'Cause folks would know that's the way things really was. No highfalutin make-believe. None a that. It'd be kinda like a history book, like real life."

- Johnny Moss, as quoted in *Fast Company* by Jon Bradshaw, 1975

"The counterattack calls for the greatest skill, the most perfect planning and the most delicate execution of all fighting techniques. It uses all the main techniques...Besides a mastery of techniques, the counterattack requires exact timing, unerring judgement and cool, calculating poise. It means careful thought, daring execution and sure control. It is the greatest art in fighting, the art of the champion."

- Bruce Lee, as quoted in *Tao of Jeet Kune Do*, 1975

"Lou Brock...was the symbol...of great base stealing. But today...I am... the greatest...of all time. Thank you."

- Rickey Henderson, after surpassing Lou Brock for the most Stolen Bases in Major League Baseball history, 1991

- 3 -

Table of Contents

Forward

Ed Chiaramonte's combination of a well-researched history lesson, thought-provoking tale of man versus machine, and insanely-detailed synopsis on what makes the greatest of anything proves to be an enjoyable read.

I've known Ed since 2007, when he moved back from England to the United States and we started working together. It didn't take long for the topic of poker and our shared interest to come up, to which we then started playing together in local games in our small Connecticut town. This was a time when poker interest was at a peak, but poker skills among the masses was not. Shortly after that we formed the Easton Series of Poker, which, while maintaining the friendly home-game ambiance, also included policing of games, mixing it up with special tournaments and awards (like the coveted Chip Reese Card, which goes to the winner of each of our special non Texas Hold Em tournaments), and lots of bookkeeping of leaderboards and other advanced stats. So far we've played tens of thousands of hands, over one hundred tournament games across ten-plus years, several trips to the World Series of Poker, and even transitioned to online games during the Coronavirus pandemic of 2020.

Ed's attention in managing the detailed records of our league make the first third of this book a great factual read of Johnny Moss's life and poker career. He's clearly always had an interest in the history of poker, with he and I sitting at the same table at Binion's in 2018 when he started talking to one of the historic Las Vegas dealers about his interactions with Johnny Moss over the years. It was fun to watch him eating up every bit of knowledge and folklore that he heard, like a kid in a candy store. The second third of the book leverages Ed's storytelling ability. His creative side comes out here with a unique storyline that will not only be eye-opening to poker players but includes a lesson for a larger audience, specifically those who will be faced with dealing with automation or machine learning in the future (i.e. all of us). The final third of the book leverages poker as its backdrop but will serve as a great conversational piece when debating the greatest of all time in any endeavor and the potential sacrifices that may come at striving for such greatness. The framework that is laid out is the most extensive I've seen on the topic and I'm sure will be talked about in sports bars and casinos for a long time to come.

Enjoy the stories!

Adam Lee

Co-Founder of the Easton Series of Poker

Ed Chiaramonte (and shirt) after winning the Easton Series of Poker

Tournament of Champions, Easton CT, 2017

Chapter 5 :

More Chips

He knew he was already dead. He wasn't surprised to find himself here, though, given his profession's somewhat obligatory and often reoccurring dealings with the devil. Someone must have negotiated a deal with old Lucifer and paid a very high re-entry fee to bring him back. Sure, the proverbial Ace he kept up his sleeve probably helped, as that's what it's for, right: one more shot at a better hand. He was wise enough to know he was brought back for a reason, and that reason was likely that *he* was Johnny Moss.

Chapter 8.5 :

Shootout at the Rio

With his pondering, the game had paused momentarily, likely for less than a minute, though it seemed much longer than that.

"Take your time, Johnny" said Tomas. "The computer here doesn't get impatient. It doesn't mind how long you take and it doesn't get angry. It doesn't behave irrationally, like perhaps you or other old gamblers may have done in the past."

Was this a dig from the sharply dressed engineer to the elderly Texan? Johnny appeared to notice the comment given the eyebrow raise and stare at Tomas, but his face didn't yet reveal his next move.

Section 1 :

History / First Buy-In

Chapter 1 :

Kinda Like A History Book, Like Real Life

Every story about Johnny Moss starts with either the hand against Nick the Greek or the inaugural World Series of Poker. Some say that the first may never have happened and that the second has an element that makes it almost unbelievable as well, specifically in how that tournament ended. Regardless of the truth behind either, both are interwoven into the fabric of America's true national pastime. As rare as finding an American who has not heard of Walt Disney, one would be hard pressed to find a local of the fifty states or beyond that has not picked up a deck of playing cards and at least dabbled in the game where Aces beat Kings, asked the question if Straights beat Flushes, or wondered what value to place on the Joker if lucky enough to receive that magical card. From playing at your grandmother's card table, to your best friend's house for all of the loose change you could muster losing, to gaining enough "big money" experience to feel that you have least have a shot of going professional after watching the 1998 film *Rounders*, the game is part of our history. Is it really important if the stories of Johnny Moss, much like our own, contain elements of exaggeration or perhaps as the Sunscreen essay of 1997 by Mary Schmich more eloquently puts it about advice/nostalgia, as "fishing the past from the disposal, wiping it off, painting over the ugly parts and recycling it for more than it's worth"? The purpose of any good story is to command attention, followed by reflection, and then inspire action. Stories of Johnny Moss, whether grounded in truth or legend, have likely inspired hard work, aspirations of a better future built upon concentration in a craft, and perhaps a bit of gambling.

Before we re-tell abbreviated accounts of those stories that you may have heard as well as embark on another tale that you definitely have *not* heard, let's set the stage for providing some background of who John Hardie Moss Junior was. Tough times hit early for the young boy born in a small racially-segregated town in Texas in 1907, with his father losing his job as deputy sheriff job shortly after Johnny was born, forcing the family to gather up their belongings into a covered wagon and head west. Not shortly after, Johnny's mother died of a burst appendix and his father had to have his leg amputated after a telephone pole fell on it and the gangrene set it. Realizing how poor his family was, Johnny started buying newspapers at fractions of a cent and sold them at a few pennies each, turning a profit that he donated to the family bankroll. It was the start of that summer after graduating from the second grade that his formal education had to end, as spending time earning money was more important to his family's wellbeing than learning reading, writing and arithmetic. The best location for selling newspapers was at a local domino parlor, where he negotiated the right to sell papers inside the establishment for the small fee of a free newspaper to the owner. It was here that Johnny was first exposed to gambling and real money.

Another early job of his was helping to communicate messages between companies. Weird as it sounds in the twenty-first century, companies used to communicate to each other via sending encrypted codes. Several boys competed to be the messenger of these codes from one company to another, with the fastest to understand the Morse Code type clicks the one to win the job. Johnny was usually the quickest at interpreting the machine's meaning, winning the most jobs. His ability to understand the dots and dashes of the machine's language would be beneficial to him in another life.

While selling newspapers at the dominos parlor, he also learned to play dominos. For those who have never played, the game of dominos has an element of luck and skill, and when Johnny learned that outthinking his opponent meant he could win more money to support his family, he put more emphasis on learning the game. From domino parlor to local cardroom, Johnny's first job related to poker was when he begged for a job in catching cheaters. Cheating was prevalent throughout the history of poker, though as the game evolved from Mississippi riverboats and the Wild West to more legitimate private cardrooms, the owners increased their chances of greater revenue if their games were considered fair to all. Johnny learned about many of the tricks of cheaters at his time at the domino parlor and on the streets of Texas, and while no hard evidence exists of him ever cheating, he clearly knew enough to be successful at a job of calling out frauds at cards, which served to increase the reputation of the cardrooms where he was employed. It was at these cardrooms, of course, that he also started watching how the successful players were playing. Johnny worked at several cardrooms both as a young man as well as in his older years. He went from being employed as a watchdog for crime to the manager of some of these cardrooms, with these jobs being a good source of income. He was also getting good enough at playing cards to have that be an even bigger source of his income. Like most males of his generation, he felt a strong obligation to take care of his family financially. As time went on, he became the primary breadwinner for his father's household, though never felt a sense of pride about this, just more a feeling that he was doing what he was meant to be doing, with his family benefiting from his hard work and dedication to his field.

At the age of eighteen, Johnny married Virgie Ann Mouser, who as one would probably expect today and definitely expect back then, wasn't thrilled that her husband's primary occupation was that of a card player. They were married nonetheless. Upon their daughter's birth the following year, Johnny was forced to help the doctor home-deliver her, vowing never to have another child after witnessing first-hand that experience. His biography notes that it wasn't he or his wife that named their first and only child, but Johnny's father instead. I'm not sure my wife would have let my father name our first born, so perhaps those were different times...

After that, Johnny's career path took him on the road. Lucrative poker games were found throughout Texas and that part of the country, where rich oil men didn't mind splashing around their easily-earned money at a game of poker. Despite a slight redirection into the Navy in the early nineteen-forties, Johnny spent the middle of the twentieth century playing in various poker cash games and trying to be safe. While winning was a clear priority for him, the greater one was staying alive. Many games were often hijacked, some by local crooks, others by professionals wearing masks carrying sawed-off shotguns. Later in his career the government posed a threat, both from the Internal Revenue Service and sometimes by Federal Bureau of Investigation officers who had no issues attempting to take some of Johnny's earnings, as poker was illegal in Texas at the time. Johnny survived them all, often not unharmed and often without a cent for his night's work, though he kept going back for more, as this is who he was.

Despite the dangers, Johnny was great at his chosen profession. Much like today, where records of cash game winnings aren't recorded with accuracy, the history books don't include specifics of the wins and losses of his travel. Unlike today though, another reason to keep winnings from notoriety was that it kept away criminals, either those wanting to rob the games' biggest winner or hijack the entire game altogether. Bookkeeping and secrecy aside, Johnny was clearly legendary in his time. When other road gamblers knew of Johnny's presence at a game, it often meant one of two things. First, it was likely a big game, with lots to be won, so many hoped to get invited to play to take their share from the non-professionals. On the other hand, given Johnny's greatness, it often provided impetus to either stay away from the game (in fear of Johnny emptying their pockets at the table) or, for those brave souls with greatness on their minds, motivated them to come and take a shot at the man himself. Even then, it must have been a thrill to say that you won a pot versus the best player known at the time. One such story comes a bit later from a young, up-and-coming player from Longworth, Texas.

With a career spanning several decades, the late nineteen-sixties saw Johnny nearing what many would have considered to be retirement age. Already with grandchildren, his wife urged him to stop venturing from dangerous poker game to dangerous poker games and to enjoy the time with his now larger family. As she managed the family bankroll, she promised him one thousand dollars a week just to stay home, relax and become domesticated. The thought of sitting at home clearly itched at Johnny, so when word came out that Tom Moore of the Holiday Inn in Reno had invited him and many others to the First Texas Gambler's

Convention, Virgie gave Johnny her blessing to go and enjoy himself with his friends.

Chapter 2 :

This New Thing Called A "Poker Tournament"

And enjoy himself he must have. This first
convention is often described as the first poker
tournament, where after playing many different variants
of poker over an extended time, a winner was to be
declared. Perhaps by player vote or perhaps granted
him by the host of the game, Johnny was declared the
"King of Cards" and received a silver cup for the win.

In attendance at the event was one of Johnny's
childhood friends, Benny Binion. Benny's stories fill an
entire book themselves, so briefly, his history includes
being friends with Johnny from an early age and later
opening Binion's Horseshoe Casino. In seeing the
success of the First Texas Gambler's Convention, he
wanted to host an even bigger event. In 1970 he
announced the first ever World Series of Poker. Much
like the first World Series of Baseball, where in 1903
the American League team in Boston played a

geographically-close National League team in Pittsburgh, the idea of "world" was a bit ambitious, as this first poker event drew just about two handfuls of Benny's closest gambling friends. In modern poker tournaments, players pay an entry fee and receive a stack of tournament chips, which are then brought to the table. These chips cannot be exchanged for money as they just represent a percentage of the total prize pool, which is often given to the top ten to twenty percent of finishers in the tournament. That game is played until one player has all the chips, who receives the largest prize, then tiering down to the lower payouts, with the minimum prize often approximately twice the initial entry fee. In the first World Series of Poker, players brought cash to the tables and played for that money. It was a game that included several poker variants and over a few days of play, the conclusion was also something that would be unbelievable on today's tournament circuit. Legend has it that at the end of the event, the players voted on the winner, and to no one's surprise, each egotistical player voted for himself as the tournament's best player. When instructed again to vote for the best player other than himself, the unanimous vote went to Johnny Moss, who holds the distinction of winning the first ever World Series of Poker title. The following year, after the suggestion that holding a freeze-out tournament would garner more publicity, the tournament structure was changed. Players would pay five thousand dollars and be given a set amount of chips, followed by having to then play until one player had them all. Still a relatively new variant to the poker scene, No Limit Texas Hold Em would be the sole game played to determine the champion. The new structure yielded a familiar result, in that Johnny won again.

1972's Main Event started well for Johnny and he accumulated an early chip lead. Going into a hand with a Doyle Brunson still in his thirties, the older Moss got all of his money in with a Pair of Deuces on a Deuce – Seven – Nine – Ten board and Doyle already leaving the casino, when Doyle hit a higher set on the River to cripple Johnny. Despite his desire for action, Moss may have been starting to feel old. The following year in 1973 he made it deep again, playing heads-up for the Main Event title against another future Hall of Famer, Puggy Pearson. Despite his advanced age, Johnny was relentless in the match, with one writer describing his face as "transparently blank, the practiced result of fifty years of self-induced rigor mortis." Many in attendance though Johnny's best days were behind him, as his age was beginning to show and he was clearly fatigued, finally losing the heads-up battle. Again he thought of calling it quits. So what did he do at age sixty-six, but come back in 1974 to make it through the biggest field to date to face off against yet another future Hall of Famer in Crandell Addington. After about four hours of heads-up play, he won the coveted ten thousand dollar buy-in Main Event again when his Pocket Pair of Threes held up. 1974 was the first year that actual (gold) bracelets were awarded for winning an event, so it of course seems fitting that the series' first winner (where he won a huge silver cup) was also the series' first formal bracelet winner.

Even after that, when Johnny got older, many said that he was clearly in his decline in his seventies and eighties. Perhaps that was true, but then something even greater has to be said when he won a World Series of Poker event on his eighty-first birthday against the largest field of players he ever outlasted (193 adversaries entered the event) and then celebrated with the Binion family and a few other poker friends at the Sombrero Room with his wife for their fifty-fifth wedding anniversary. Rumor has it he then played cash games later that night, but more on family later. With that win, he remains the oldest World Series of Poker bracelet winner to this day. Surely he would be done playing competitively, or at least well, at eighty-one, right? This guy had something special in him, making four more Final Tables between his eighty-second and eighty-third year on earth, capping off his World Series of Poker cashes with a twelfth place finish out of 254 entrants at the age of eighty-four. A young Phil Hellmuth of age twenty-seven finished that same tournament in ninth place. When he needed to, there was clearly a reserve that only the great ones possess, and it was clear that despite aging, players young and old continued to see him as a formidable opponent while most mortals his age were content in rocking chairs watching the literal and proverbial sun set.

When discussing the great players of the World Series of Poker and of poker in general, Johnny Moss's name is intrinsically linked. Historical significance of winning poker's earliest tournaments aside, Johnny Moss was more than just poker's first "official" champion. Johnny won World Series of Poker bracelets in eight different years. Despite the tournament's fifty year history, his nine bracelets still ranks fifth among all-time bracelet winners (placing behind poker luminaries Phil Hellmuth, Doyle Brunson, Johnny Chan and Phil Ivey). Most of today's poker players start their tournament careers in their twenties (if not earlier), so nine bracelets when starting his tournament poker career in his sixties is quite an accomplishment. When most in their eighties are either resting or already laid to rest, Johnny was still cashing against fields that were likely very much younger than him.

It wasn't just that he won tournaments that made Johnny a household name in poker. Doyle Brunson, the back-to-back Main Event winner in 1976 and 1977 and proclaimed "Godfather of Poker" given not only his dominating play but also seminal book published in 1978 *How I Made Over $1,000,000 Playing Poker* (later retitled as *Super/System*), noted that if he ever had an idol in the game of poker, it was Johnny Moss. Doyle wrote another book, published in 2007 titled *My 50 Most Memorable Hands* and what do you know, the first of those fifty hands and one labelled easily the most memorable in Doyle's career came against Johnny Moss. Doyle was just entering the "Texas Circuit," which consisted of poker games taking place at various locations throughout the state. As noted earlier, Johnny was the circuit's best known player and winner, so when the up-and-coming Doyle won a huge pot against him with Jack-high, it was not only profitable for the youngster but one he wanted to advertise to show his own greatness and hand-reading ability.

Johnny Moss was also said to have been the idol of a young Stu Ungar, who first learned about the game at age sixteen when Moss won his first World Series of Poker. Ungar went on to have one of the best No Limit Texas Hold Em poker tournament careers, winning the World Series of Poker's Main Event three times (equalling Johnny's record, to which, will never be broken given the larger fields of entrants in the modern game) and supposedly winning ten out of the total thirty No Limit Texas Hold Em tournaments he entered. The best players today *cash* in about three out of ten tournaments, making Ungar's winning rate absurd.

Many consider David "Chip" Reese the best all-around poker player in history. He was perhaps the best cash game player ever and won the inaugural fifty thousand dollar buy-in H.O.R.S.E. tournament at the World Series of Poker in 2006. That tournament included mostly Limit betting, where only a pre-set amount of chips could be bet when it was a player's turn to act, as opposed to No Limit, where a player could wager any amount up to the entire amount they were sitting with) and the fifty thousand dollars was the largest of its time. Johnny Moss played with Chip many times over the years and they didn't always get along. One of Johnny's strengths in poker was the ability to read his opponent correctly and sizing his bets accordingly, in either getting his opponents to call the most when their hands were inferior or fold to bets when they actually had the better hands. These tactics were best applied in the No Limit variants of poker, whereas, Chip Reese, a Dartmouth graduate, was more of an expert in Limit variants, where math was often more important than the feel of the players that Johnny clearly had. While Johnny originally struggled with these types of games now more popular in Las Vegas, he was adaptable enough to start watching Chip Reese and others in how they approached Limit games. Johnny learned quickly, with his last five World Series of Poker bracelets coming at Limit variants of poker. When needed, he could clearly adapt to any game and situation. About the same time as Johnny's early World Series of Poker success, a young writer and martial artist named Bruce Lee penned the line: "Intelligence is sometimes defined as the capacity of the individual to adjust himself to his environment – or to adjust the environment to his needs." Johnny's ability to adjust would come in useful later.

Chapter 3 :

Legend of the Big Game #1

The controversial tale that starts Chapter One begins with a few characters, and I do mean characters in the truest sense of the word. Benny Binion, the always-cowboy-hat-wearing eventual founder of the World Series of Poker was one of them. Nick "the Greek" Dandolos, who gambled with everyone in his time and is said to have "broken" the famous racketeer Arnold Rothstein (whose infamous notoriety may be best linked to initiating the Black Sox scandal of 1919 in which the Chicago White Sox threw the [baseball] World Series) and is the other main character in this story. The legend goes that Nick wanted some big action and contacted Benny, whose casino was later known as providing the highest stakes gambling in Las Vegas, to find him a worthy opponent. Benny contacted his long time childhood friend, who just so happened to be the best poker player anyone had ever seen up to that point. Despite just finishing up a four day poker game himself, Johnny Moss hopped on a plane and made the trip north.

The game was then set up. Perhaps the game was in 1949 at the Flamingo, perhaps it was set up at Binion's Horseshoe Casino in the early nineteen-fifties (as there was no Binion's Horseshoe Casino in 1949). Perhaps there was a crowd of spectators and other players at the table, perhaps not. I updated the Johnny Moss Wikipedia page with Benny's son Jack's thoughts on the topic a few years ago, in which he tries to clarify some of the specifics of the game, though those are not important. With slight variations in the details of the story, even sceptics bet that Johnny Moss did play against Nick Dandolos. Several days into the event, where both players may have gone over twenty-four hours without sleep, *the* notable hand came up. The game was Five-Card Stud, which isn't played much anymore, though you can find a good re-enactment of it

- 40 -

in the 1965 movie *The Cincinnati Kid* with Steve
McQueen and Edward G. Robinson. The game is played
with each player receiving one card each down (that the
other player cannot see), along with one card that each
player can see. Given the relative strength of their hand
and/or the perceived strength (or weakness) of their
opponent's hand, each player is allowed to bet. In this
game, the betting was huge relative to the times.
Johnny was dealt a Nine as his hidden card and a Six
that Nick can see, while Nick received his one down-
card and the other was an Eight. After both players put
in the mandatory ante, Johnny bet a small amount,
Nick raised, and Johnny called. Johnny was then dealt
another nine, giving him a Pair of Nines, which is a
strong hand after just three cards dealt. Nick received a
Six. Regardless of what Nick's down card was, Johnny
knew he had the best hand, as his Pair of Nines could
not be beaten. Johnny bet, Nick raised, and Johnny
just called. Johnny then received a Deuce, with Nick
getting a Four. Again, Johnny was certain he had the

best hand so bet, though this time Nick just called. The final card to Johnny was a Three, changing nothing about the strength of his hand, which remained a Pair of Nines. Nick received a Jack, which given how Nick was playing the hand, wouldn't have seemed to help improve his hand. Nick surprised Johnny with a big bet after that final card, which was something he often did when he thought a big bet could scare away an opponent. Johnny, of course knowing that, as well as being able to read the board and fully understanding that the Jack was unlikely to have helped Nick's hand, raised enough to potentially win all of Nick's money if victorious. Nick called and turned over a very unlikely Jack as his down card, giving him a Pair of Jacks, which beat Johnny's Pair of Nines.

There's a line in the classic poker movie *The Cincinnati Kid* where Edward G. Robinson's character, Lancey Howard (also known as "The Man") plays the villain versus Steve McQueen's hero of Eric Stoner (also known as "The Kid"). During the final hand of their heads-up battle, The Man wins by playing a similar hand of Five Card Stud with a weak starting hand also consisting of a Jack as his down card (like Nick the Greek) along with a suited Eight. The Man risks a lot of money while clearly behind in the hand but miraculously wins with a Straight Flush on his fifth and final card, earning enough cash to break The Kid and send him away. As the final scene unfolds, he utters the debatable line pitting skill against luck: "Gets down to what it's all about, doesn't it? Making the wrong move at the right time."

The movie ends with The Kid leaving, clearly with ego deflated, likely hoping to earn a big enough bankroll to one day come back and make a run for the top spot again. In real life (or in 1949 or 1951, whenever this hand actually happened between Johnny Moss and Nick Dandolos), Johnny did not walk away the loser. Johnny understood that an opponent who was willing to gamble and take a long-shot bet for one big hand was eventually going to end a loser. He was good enough to know his opponent was not one that was willing to stop playing when he won a big pot too, so knew he had the time to make a comeback. Now even more energized after finding this weakness in his opponent, Johnny became more focused than ever. The game went on, perhaps lasting up to five months, and with slow but superior play, Johnny went on to dominate Nick. One can be sure that when it was time to end the game, Nick did not know what hit him, as supposedly he was down more money than was ever wagered in poker. Some estimates suggest than the total sum that Johnny won was between two and three million dollars, which would be the equivalent of between twenty five and thirty five million dollars today. With the monumental loss about to be finalized, Nick uttered the famous line of "Mister Moss, I have to let you go," after he in fact had nothing left to play with. Johnny Moss had adjusted to his opponent's tendencies and via superior play, emerged victorious.

Chapter 4 :

Agin' Ain't Easy

Despite unprecedented tournament success in his later years, Johnny Moss didn't age particularly well. While he stayed married and had several grandchildren and great grandchildren from his daughter Eleoweese's family, family-time for this elderly man wasn't demonstrated in the traditional manner. Financially, his family was doing fine given the investments in real estate that his wife had started, namely in purchasing two apartment buildings in Odessa, Texas. Emotionally, he may not have been the most "present" member of his family. He had held several positions at different casinos in Las Vegas over the years, mostly as card room managers, and didn't seem to be home in Texas a lot. Not only was Johnny Moss a card room manager for many of the famous casinos in Las Vegas, but he was often an attraction.

Poker chips were minted with his name engraved, labelled "John Moss / World Champion Poker Player" to attract players to come see or even play with the living legend. While Johnny didn't mind taking tourists' money, he wasn't the most gracious host or boss to those in the cardroom. Just ask Keith over at Binion's to tell you a few stories, of how Johnny fired him after being dealt a few bad hands. David Heyden, who later went on to a respectable tournament career, was once fired as a dealer himself by Johnny for playing at a nearby casino and not the one managed by Moss. Despite Oklahoma Johnny Hale leveraging Johnny's celebrity to start the Seniors World Championship of Poker and induct Moss into the Senior's Hall of Fame, he described him as not-quite deserving of the Grand Old Man title that the positive moniker implied. Barry Greenstein quotes in his book, *Ace On The River*, that one time when Johnny Moss was losing in a game, the wife of a player who had just died called him and asked if he would contribute to the funeral. He was then quoted to have said that he was losing his money to live people, and didn't have any for the dead. Doyle Brunson seems to have made it a personal goal to not age like Johnny Moss, as in his most senior years he wasn't playing his best poker or managing his bankroll well.

Despite what was still likely a very sharp mind from time to time, the wear and tear of life on the road was wearing him thin. Even the travel from Texas to Nevada grew tiresome. Early in his eighty-eighth year he suffered a stroke at a car wash, to which he was then taken away from Binion's and Las Vegas by his daughter to and return home to Odessa to spend his final days. At the Medical Center Hospital in town, Johnny actually remembered when the doctor came into his room and called out his time of death. "Wait a minute," he thought. "I'm not supposed to remember that."

Section 2 :

Rebirth / Rebuy

Chapter 6 :

Rebirth

Of course the narrative doesn't end here.
Throughout his life, Johnny knew that his only
formidable adversary was his own humanity. He had
character flaws like the rest of us. He knew that he was
getting old and wasn't able to adjust to the players and
new poker games that were being introduced as quickly
as he did even as a man in his sixties. Medicine in the
last years of the twentieth century wasn't ready to bring
the eighty-eight year old back from the near dead. Nor
were other "higher order" powers likely looking down
favorably at him, as the Dealer in the sky probably
didn't see enough good being done by this man to keep
him around any longer. Johnny also figured that his life
as a poker player wasn't the most noble one looked
upon by the angels, reasoning that his overall life had
already skewed luckier than most, so figured his luck

had finally fun out and was ready to cash in all his chips.

But while the figurative Man upstairs may have had enough of Johnny Moss gambling stories, perhaps there was another reason to keep him around? What if it was his destiny to really push the limits of high success, temporarily postponing the inevitable fall due to the frailty of the human condition? Could keeping him around still teach us something? Surely just a bit more time for a single soul wouldn't upset the eternal balance of those still living and those whose chips were lost after their final hand turned over and their losing revelation presented.

And just like that, Johnny Moss didn't leave us at age eighty-eight on December 16th, 1995. Instead he found himself alive and well, feeling much more youthful than he had last remembered. He still felt like the Grand Old Man of Poker with all of his experience intact, but many years younger. He looked and felt sixty-three, the year he won the inaugural World Series of Poker. The last thing he remembered craving before his first death was a poker game, so the obvious next step in this rebirth was probably going to be to find some action.

And that's where I come in. I was one of the poor souls that Mister Moss used to devour for dinner at the poker tables. Like countless others, I was one of the many local poker champions across the world who did well in our home games or nearby casinos. As an organizer of many home games, my invite list included over sixty individuals from all walks of life, ranging from marketing researchers to lawyers to electricians to septic tank pumpers to HVAC technicians to veterinarians. We played monthly No Limit Texas Hold Em tournaments for sixty dollars in someone's basement or dining room, often getting two or three tables going. During the Coronavirus pandemic of 2020, our games moved online for a while, where for forty dollars we hosted a weekly mix of No Limit Texas

Hold Em, Eight Game (which is a mix of eight different poker disciplines) or my personal favorite, Pot Limit Omaha High Low Eight or Better. Anyway, Johnny Moss regularly took on local champs like me at either the cash games or the tournament tables and at best sent us home with some stories to tell of how we were outplayed by one of the masters, or at worst, vowing that we had lost more than we wanted during the games and that we would never touch another deck of cards again. Stu Ungar, the only other three-time World Series of Poker Main Event winner alongside Johnny Moss summed it up nicely: "Think about what it's like sitting at a poker table with people whose only goal is to cut your throat, take your money, and leave you out back talking to yourself about what went wrong inside. That probably sounds harsh. But that's the way it is at the poker table. If you don't believe me, then you're the lamb that's going off to the slaughter." I was a big fish in a small pond but a fluffy cotton creature when playing against the likes of a true World Champion. I was also a bit of a poker historian, so I was well aware who Johnny Moss was and his place in the poker pantheon of greats, which I supposed was one of the reasons I ended up meeting Johnny upon his rebirth.

"Welcome to 2020, Mister Moss. It's great to have you back."

"Good to be back," was his quick and somewhat uncertain answer. He looked around, trying to take it all in very quickly. I couldn't quite say how we both got there, but there we were, in an indistinct field, perhaps behind a school or community center. The grass was a faded bronze, as the summer on the outskirts of downtown Las Vegas had already begun to erase the greenness that was likely here just a few weeks ago. After looking around at his surroundings, Johnny then appeared clearly surprised by his own appearance, as he reviewed himself as if he weren't sure any of this was real. He first looked at his hands, which were clearly old, and despite the nearly seventy years of marriage to his wife, still was not wearing a wedding ring. He was wearing a pair of comfortable-looking dress shoes, neatly pressed light-brown dress pants and a light blue sweater hanging over a thin dark blue mock turtleneck. He checked that he was indeed wearing his familiar black glasses. Of the hair he had left, its silver shade graced the sides and back of his head in that typical older-male balding pattern. To me, he looked exactly as I would have pictured him. He was clearly flesh and blood again, with no ghostlike qualities. With this humanity though, came a regality that he likely carried in his first life as well. Sometimes people stand out in a crowd, and for no apparent reason, even a casual observer could sense the greatness of the man. I had never met him in person, as my own poker career started after 1995, and only viewed pictures of him from the internet, books and old poker magazines, but his appearance seemed to fit the bill of how he appeared in the early years of the nineteen-seventies. He smelled like a grandfather would if he were about to attend a family wedding, which had the peculiar effect on me of revealing his age but also demonstrating that he still had some pride about how he was perceived by others. After taking a brief overview of himself, he also took a good look at me. Just like he had been able to read opponents at the poker table, I'm sure he made judgements about me just by my short utterance, facial expression, posture, gray Nike sneakers, torn khaki shorts, Berkshire Hathaway t-shirt depicting a rainbow pattern over the shape of Nebraska, and probably a few other variables. He quickly realized that I was not the reason he was brought back to life. "So who's the best poker player in the world today?"

"Wow, good question" was my first response, though before I could give the answer any thought, I was amazed that this was his first question. Here's a guy who has just emerged from the netherworld and the first thing he's looking for is the top competition. Was competing truly his raison d'être? What would *my* first question have been? I would have hoped it would

be something like "Can you take me to see my

grandkids?" but family didn't appear to be top of mind.

Then again, perhaps he had the foresight to know that

he wasn't being brought back from the dead to attend

the latest family barbecue.

I then continued. "Phil Ivey is widely considered

the best all-around player in the world, though hasn't

been playing in the United States as much lately due to

some recent issues surrounding the morality and

legality of beating the casino in other card games. Plus

the games in Macau are supposedly even better than

Las Vegas. Phil Hellmuth has the most World Series of

Poker bracelets with fifteen and is still a great

tournament player, though doesn't appear to be much

of a high-stakes cash-game player. Doyle Brunson is

still alive and well, though given he's almost as old as

you (eighty-seven) when you, uh, left us the first time,

he doesn't play as much as he used to either and

recently retired from tournament poker. Fedor Holz is

one of the best players now in terms of really leveraging GTO play..."

"Ah, Doyle. He was a good player. He always liked tellin' that story 'bout how he beat me out of a hand with Jack High. I'll have to look him up if I get the time."

"I actually met Doyle once myself," I somewhat interrupted "at a book signing of *Super System 2*, in New York. You're mentioned in that book. I even got a picture with him. I'll have to get a picture with you..."

Ed Chiaramonte and Doyle Brunson,

Barnes & Noble, New York, NY, 2005.

Phil Ivey and Ed Chiaramonte,

Rio All-Suite Hotel and Casino, Las Vegas, NV, 2012.

"And Phil Hellmuth. I remember him bein' a cocky kid when he won the Main Event in 1989. I know he took the game seriously."

"Yes, he definitely plays well against big fields of recreational players but hasn't had the same success in No Limit Texas Hold Em against the top players. When it comes to cash games..."

And he interrupted again. The stories I had heard was that he wasn't a man with the most gracious manners, but I was still in awe of him. "What's this GTO thing you mentioned?"

"Oh, GTO. That stands for Game Theory Optimal. According to Wikipedia (which is sort of like a set of encyclopedias, but online), Game Theory is the study of mathematical models of strategic interaction among rational decision-makers. According to MasterClass (an online set of courses hosted by masters in their field, like Daniel Negreanu and Phil Ivey), Game Theory Optimal (GTO) poker is an umbrella-term players use to describe the holy grail of No-Limit Texas Hold Em playing strategy, by which you become unexploitable to your opponents and improve your win-rate. It's quite popular right now in that the top players use online solvers to calculate the ideal play against their opponent's range of hands and then devise the best plays with it, so that even if their opponent knew they were playing GTO poker, there would be nothing they could do to counter it. Oh, before I go on, I guess I should explain what 'online' is to you as I'm not sure you got to experience that your first time around..."

Again, sort of with an interruption, Johnny didn't seem too interested in what "online" meant but instead his interest clearly piqued when I was describing an unexploitable strategy. "*People* actually play this style of poker?," asking with already somewhat of a clear understanding that there was a delineation of what was possible by machines versus the human mind.

It's almost as if he had started putting the pieces together in his head, trying to figure out what he had to do in order to compete today. "Well, no Mister Moss, people *try* to play GTO, but the calculations are so intense that it requires a lot of computing hours to devise optimal play. Players do a lot of studying today trying to understand what the computers are telling them the optimal plays are so that they can bring that learning to the actual tables when they play. Now, on top of that, there are super-computers that leverage Artificial Intelligence, or AI, that not only play GTO poker, but take into account their opponent's tendencies but then can also devise strategies that are exploitative against them...."

"No computer can beat a real poker player if he knows what he's doin'," Johnny said almost nonchalantly, but also with a seriousness that made it seem like it was going to be a hard argument to win against him if I tried to counter, which I did.

"Sorry, Mister Moss, that train has passed. Since you've been gone (the first time), computers have beaten the best chess players, the best Jeopardy! players...oh, Jeopardy!, it's a trivia game with a bit of wagering...and top poker players. Computers, or AI, have beaten top players in heads-up poker play as well as six-handed tournament play. On one hand, the computer plays Game Theory Optimal poker so that no matter the strategy played against it, it can't lose in the long run. It randomizes its play to some extent so that it's not predictable, though at the same time, knows the exact probabilities of plays that it should use to mix up its betting, calling, raising and folding to be unexploitable. For example, if it always bet two-thirds the pot when it Flops a Flush Draw, it might become predictable. It might suggest instead that it bet two-thirds the pot half the time, one-third the pot one quarter of the time, and check one quarter of the time. Related, if its human opponents show any weaknesses or imperfect tendencies, which, let's face it, we all have, it picks up on those and moves forward with those exploitative strategies to win even more. For instance, if it notices its opponents fold too much, the computer will bluff more. If they call too much, the computer bluffs less and value-bets more. The smartest companies in the world, like IBM, Google, and PiMS, have taken these concepts so far that computers can play these games perfectly."

"Why are these companies creatin' these computers to beat poker games? Do they get to win money versus players?" seemed like a fair question for Johnny to ask, to perhaps gauge these companies' motivation to create such computers in the first place.

"When a company sets up a game and then has its computer beat top players in their respective field, the sponsoring company gets a ton of positive public relations. Investors then want a piece of the latest technology, as they then believe that it represents the future of society, in that it will find efficiencies that will help other companies make more money if they leverage their technology. Some debate if technology will completely diminish the role of man in the workplace, though I still think that's a bit of science fiction that will never come completely true. Anyway, when investors who believe that the company's technology will be purchased by others, they buy a lot of stock, then the value of that stock then goes up, making both the investors and the big shareholders (who are typically senior employees at the company) all get rich. Often times, even the human loser who competed in the face-off with the computer benefits, as everyone wants to know what it was like competing in that arena, and he's given high-paid speaking engagements. Garry Kasparov might have been your equivalent in the world of chess. He is widely regarded as the best chess player of all time, though after eventually falling to a computer in a well-publicized tournament in 1997, even he now admits that he has no chance of winning a single game against the super-computers of today."

"Take me to this PiMS."

Well now this seemed exciting! Given the six degrees of separation between everyone, it didn't take long for me to sift through my LinkedIn contacts and make the connections needed so that Johnny could be introduced to the top brass at Pivotal Intelligence / Mind Structures.

"Mister Johnny Moss, it's a pleasure to meet you," Tomas Christopher said as he met the legend. "Your reputation precedes you, as one of the pioneers of the modern game of poker and one of its historically greatest players."

"The pleasure, I assure you, is mine. So you invented PiMS?"

"Ha, not quite. PiMS actually started during World War II when computers were just starting to get off the ground. The company isn't a big consumer-facing brand like some of the others that are more well-known today, but most of them end up leveraging our thinking to make their products and innovations even stronger. Since we started in 1944, the company has made numerous advances in artificial intelligence and machine learning. Machines can now compete in 'games' that were previously thought to be the pinnacle of human intelligence, such as chess, Jeopardy!, poker and Go. I head up PiMS's equivalent to IBM's Watson project, which is one of the leaders in this type of intelligence, so get to lead the thinking of the brightest engineers and data scientists that create and fine-tune the machines to not only compete in games like this but to further the development of medicine and healthcare, automate complex processes, and lots of other more practical uses."

"Team of engineers and data scientists, huh? Interestin'..."

"Well, yes, Johnny, I head up the side of PiMS that actually creates the machine, though we also have a marketing department. Back in your day, poker wasn't that exciting to watch, as viewers had no way of seeing players' concealed cards, and most hands ended with them not having to be revealed. With advances in other forms of technology, namely when Henry Orenstein patented the tiny cameras at the poker table that would allow for an audience to view the players' otherwise-concealed cards, poker has moved from being a very boring game to watch to a very exciting television experience. Viewership for the World Series of Poker and other big tournaments are now televised, with viewers joining the excitement of seeing if their favorite players were going win, what outrageous bluffs would be made, and how the luck of the cards could change fortunes. Now as you may know, despite several decisive wins at heads-up poker and six-handed play, artificial intelligence has yet to have been highlighted via a televised headline event against a true legend of the game. Not only would poker fans want to see this match, but general market viewers who want to witness the latest chapter in the man versus machine saga would tune in. From our perspective, it also would bring in millions of dollars in advertising and sponsorship for the event. If we were able to create a program that pitted arguably the best poker player of all-time against our latest poker-playing machine, that would be huge. Am I right to assume that you would be up for such a contest?"

"I think that's why I'm here." Johnny replied with a slight questioning in his voice, but also the sternest confidence. "I can't remember ever turnin' down a big game, whether it was against Nick the Greek, Doyle Brunson, Stu Ungar, or any of them big oil men in Texas."

"Great. There will be some paperwork to complete so that we have everything in writing that we're on the same page with expectations, but this should be fun. As you might have heard, 2020 was an interesting year for all of us, and the poker world wasn't spared either. We had a global pandemic, a level of social unrest that had not been seen in over a generation, severe effects from climate change, and a political climate that has separated the country like never before. The poker world has been impacted too, with the World Series of Poker at the Rio cancelled this summer, replaced by an online series. The game we're about to host will take people's minds off all of that for a while and bring back some of that normalcy to poker players, seeing a live game played at the Rio again. We'll make it a big deal. As it will be televised, we'll also have advertising dollars to compensate for the prize, so there will be no entry fee that you have to put up yourself. My guess is that based on the advertising we'll generate, our prizes will likely be something to the effect of one million dollars to the winner and two hundred fifty thousand dollars to the loser."

"Good," was the response from Johnny, which came out as a clear understanding of what he was being told, but given an almost unnoticeable pause before he started his next line, it was clear he wasn't just blindly accepting the terms without making sure they were indeed at least mutually beneficial. "I'll sign your papers, no problem. I can think of only two conditions myself though. You say the computer does all the thinkin' and then spits out what it thinks the best move is, right?"

"Yes, that's right. The machine outputs a decision and assigns it a confidence level that it is the correct move."

"Well, since I've never played this modern internet-type of poker before and sure ain't used to playin' against a computer, is it ok if I ask that I be sittin' across from another human bein', who makes the final call of whether or not to accept the action that the computer suggests?"

"Uh, yeah, sure, that shouldn't be a problem. I can even do that, as a representative of the team of engineers who have worked on the AI. Now, to be clear, you won't be playing against me, per se. I'll just be taking advice from the computer and doing what it recommends. I'm not foolish enough to try to play you myself. I really don't have much of a poker face!"

"Ok, good," Johnny smirked, without acknowledging the humor or compliment intended by Tomas's last response. "I had one other thought. At any point in this game, can I name the stakes?"

"What do you mean, stakes? Just like the World Series of Poker in 1971, we're thinking of playing a tournament-style freeze-out, where the winner will be the one who eventually ends up with all the chips, with a defined first and second place finisher. Will that work for you?"

"Well, that's nice and all, but I'd like to add in a little of the cash-game element to it as well. Sorta like side-action. The cash tends to make the game more excitin'...which I'm sure your television audience would appreciate."

"Uh, ok, sure. I'm sure that wouldn't be a problem, as I'm sure we could find some petty cash in PiMS's change drawer to meet your needs." With a grin, the response was clearly meant to indicate that PiMS could match any amount that the Grand Old Man of Poker could fathom playing for.

Papers were signed, a date for just two weeks from then was agreed to, and it seemed like both sides were on their way to an event that would prove their points of superiority of man versus machine.

Chapter 7 :

Preparation

We left the PiMS office and Johnny was antsy with places to go. Most of his contemporaries were no longer living, though he had two names he wanted to catch up with. One was Doyle Brunson and the other Phil Ivey. When I dropped him off at The Bellagio for a meeting with Doyle, he didn't want me to follow him in. I was staying at the much cheaper but still elegant Sahara Hotel & Casino a bit further down the strip, so headed there until I heard back from him. Originally opened in 1952, I wondered if Johnny had ever visited the Sahara during his early years in Las Vegas. The appreciation of nostalgia was one that I know many people hold dear, and here I was living the dream, not only spending my days in a renovated version of an old classic but being the chaperone to a renovated classic poker player. After a short nap, I was awoken by the phone in the room by someone at the front desk, who alerted me that a Mister Johnny Moss was ready to be picked up at the Bellagio. Fair enough that Johnny didn't have my mobile number and of course he didn't have a phone himself to Uber over. I thought it somewhat ironic that someone whose idea of modern technology may have been the telephone was about to embark in a contest versus the most modern of technologies.

"So what was it like meeting, I mean, seeing Doyle again?"

"It was different" he replied, somewhat impressed by the time-travel aspect of his rebirth. "Throughout Doyle's life, I was always the Grand Old Man of Poker. I was the one he chased all throughout the South West, lookin' to get a game with me, the old master, tryin' to learn what made me the legend that I was. He was the new kid on the block, the up-and-comer, tryin' to show the world that he was number one. And he clearly did ok for himself, history'll show that. But now, seein' him for the first time as an old-timer himself, it was interestin' seeing each other as peers for the first time."

"Wow, that is an interesting perspective. Grandfathers don't often get to talk to their grandchildren when they become grandfathers" was the analogy that left my tongue after hearing Johnny's perspective.

"I actually visited Doyle at his house when we all thought he was on his death bed. Had a lump in his throat when he was younger that the docs all said was gonna kill him. I'm sure my visit had nothin' to do with it, but he recovered after that, so it was good to see that he also got to live to a ripe old age."

"I guess your visit back then showed the mutual respect you had for each other, even while you were both adversaries, as well as your visit today."

"I did have to confront him 'bout one thing though. He often wrote 'bout the hand where he beat me with Jack High. As you probably remember, a young Doyle and I and were playing in a big cash game in Brenham, Texas. Three of us got to see a cheap Flop of King-Eight-Seven and there was six hundred dollars in the pot. The first guy bets three hundred eighty dollars with a King in his hand. I called the bet with a Six- Five, as I have a lot of outs with the Straight Draw and Doyle calls with a Jack-Ten, giving him overcards to the second card on the Flop and a gutshot draw to the best Straight. The next card on the Turn is a Deuce, which we all checked. The last card is a Three on the River. The first guy with the King checked, and knowin' that he wasn't that strong, I made a big bet of four thousand dollars. I knew Doyle couldn't have been that strong either, as if he was, he woulda bet the Turn to protect his hand. Well, Doyle had been watchin' me for a while now and made a great read on me, callin' my bet, which scared away the first guy, who couldn't have

- 82 -

thought his weak King was good enough to win the hand. Y'unnderstand now, Doyle made a great read on me and made a lot of money in that hand. And, I appreciate that Doyle also noted in several of his writin's that despite me losing that big hand, I also played well enough to break even that game. That was his way of sayin' I was still a great player, despite of course makin' himself seem like the better one for winnin' that huge pot. But what Doyle never did write about, and believe me, he knew, was that I used the legend of that hand many times to make more than a hundred times that pot in my career. Once other players thought they knew that old Johnny's overbets were possibly bluffs, I was called more often than a switchboard operator at American Telephone and Telegraph."

While it took me longer than it should have to appreciate his last analogy, I definitely could appreciate his point of view on Doyle wanting to accept the praise for making a great call, which had to have made Johnny feel a bit embarrassed at the time.

"I lost alot of money playin' poker. I minded losin' it, of course, but what really bothered me was when the other guy didn't win the right way. Some celebrate at the table, jump up and down like they won the Main Event. Some like Doyle gotta go and write about it. Just win the money and act like it's not the first time you raked in a pot."

"I'm a fan of that philosophy, Mister Moss. And I try to promote that at the home games I manage. That said, there have been stories of times that you weren't the best loser. I was actually at Binion's in 2018 and was talking to a dealer there named Keith, who said he used to work for you when you were managing one of the cardrooms in Las Vegas. While he said that Stu Ungar was awful to deal with as a player at his tables, you once fired him over a bad run-out of cards. What's your view on that story?"

"Well, I ain't never claimed to be perfect."

Ed Chiaramonte and "Keith the Dealer,"

Binion's Gambling Hall, Las Vegas, NV, 2018.

Ha, fair enough. "And you also saw Phil Ivey while you were there?"

"Yeah, I saw him." With this, despite not being the best at being able to read people, it was clear Johnny was holding that conversation close to his vest, as not to reveal that hand, yet. I drove him back to the Sahara, though he didn't want to check in yet to the room I reserved for him, instead telling me was going to take a walk for a while. It was late, though with all the life around Las Vegas at night, I knew he would be safe. I didn't know of anywhere else he needed to go, but especially given he was a bit quiet on the ride back from The Bellagio, I didn't want to pry into anything I wasn't supposed to be aware of yet.

Chapter 8 :

The Big Game #2

If you've ever been to the Rio during the World
Series of Poker, you understand the electricity that goes
through the building in late Spring and early Summer.
There are several huge rooms where the tournaments
take place, holding around five hundred poker tables.
During any single day there are often multiple
tournaments going on at once, neatly divided into
different sections of the different rooms, with the
constant movement of dealers switching from table to
table, players sitting down with high hopes of a gold
bracelet, players leaving with dreams busted, and of
course the unceasing shuffling of chips, with their
rhythmic frequencies the unofficial soundtrack to any
poker setting. The unofficial "official" soundtrack to the
World Series of Poker is Ennio Morricone's *Ecstasy of
Gold*, written first for the famous Spaghetti Western

starring Clint Eastwood, *The Good, the Bad and the Ugly*, which now plays at the start of several of the events. Both the western theme as well as the thought of gold is fitting, given the geography of the event and the token bracelet given out to each event's winner, along with a very large dollar figure. With the official 2020 World Series of Poker not taking place at the Rio due to the pandemic, these familiar sounds were missing.

What was not missing, as they were much easier to arrange than setting up a plethora of poker tables, were the huge banners hanging throughout the Rio's rafters of each of the World Series of Poker Main Events' champions. Johnny Moss has a banner alongside the other winners of the now fifty Main Events that have been held. With that, it seemed fitting to hold this event, of man versus machine, also being held at the Rio, right below the Johnny Moss banner. While the "final tables" of events are typically showcased in a different area of the casino floor, the decision was made to set up the stage where Johnny's banner hung. As with anything made for television, lights and cameras surrounded the standard poker table, with seats set up on the other side of the camera much like the staging of one of the heavyweight fights often held at the MGM Grand just a few miles away.

World Series of Poker Main Event Champion Banner

Rio All-Suite Hotel and Casino, Las Vegas, 2018.

Johnny had never seen his banner hung at the Rio, as the World Series of Poker moved all but the final table of its Main Event in 2005 to the Rio from Binion's Horseshoe. I would have thought both the enormity of his banner as well as the just the size of the room would have at least sparked at brow furrow by him, though Johnny seemed more focused in getting comfortable in his new surroundings. In novel surroundings of his past, he would have to search the walls or under the table for mirrors to reflect cards to other players or even search the walls and ceilings for spies who would be relaying information to other players based on what they saw. He would have to check the decks for marked cards, whose scratches or slightest of man-made imperfections could give away valuable information about what a player held or what was about to be dealt. In this game, Johnny had to get comfortable with the modern hole cam, which in this case would showcase Johnny's hand to viewers only after the hand was completely over. Even the seat he was asked to sit in was nothing like even Benny Binion's early ideas of luxury at his casino, with the now ergonomically designed and stylish gaming chairs of today taking a bit of getting used to for the old man.

PiMS did its best to make sure Johnny was comfortable. Not only did he get a nice chair, but a complimentary meal before the match and snacks and beverages during. Almost similar to a prize fight, there was even a warm-up, so that Johnny was ready when the lights went on. They played a few practice hands just so all of them would know what to expect. Just like a typical live heads-up match, Johnny was set up on one end of a large poker table and Tomas the other, which was even more fitting for 2020 given the social distancing that became the norm. And right next to Tomas, in its own chair, was the computer.

The PiMS computer was given the nickname UNGAR MMXX. Not unlike one of its predecessors, IBM's Watson, who was named after its founder and first CEO, the name chosen for the computer playing this match was also significant. Stu Ungar and Johnny Moss are tied for the most World Series of Poker Main Event wins with three, so the latest battle of man versus machine could also be looked at as a heads-up match between the two biggest names in poker's biggest tournament. Like the person it was named after, UNGAR MMXX wasn't especially bulky or huge, being placed on a regular chair and about the size of an average person. Despite its smaller size, there was definitely something intimidating about the machine. Its sleek silver color seemed to coat its bullet-proof-looking exterior. There wasn't a lot of flair on the machine, with just a few ports for connections and a few LED lights at what appeared to be its front. While Johnny had seen computers in his day, he had likely never seen anything like this one.

The one new feature that UNGAR MMXX added to its already strong arsenal of tactics was its facial coding software. Not only was its computing power enough to provide game theory optimal outputs balanced with exploitative play based on its opponents' tendencies, but equipped with a camera that was able to view facial expressions, breathing patterns, pulse rate and hand motions, it was able to combine these typically-human behaviors into its algorithms to come up with the best recommended decisions.

At the physical table where they sat, both Johnny and Tomas each had huge stacks of clay Paulson poker chips in front of them to bet, which represented the tournament chips they would be playing with. To keep with the feel that this was a real poker game, there was also an actual human dealer (wearing a mask), sitting between them, who dealt special cards that were RFID enabled. This was a relatively new technology used so that not only could the hole cam literally see Johnny's physical cards, but the computer would be able to "see" its own cards. The computer was not of course ever privy to the cards that were dealt to Johnny unless they were revealed at the end of a hand. Tomas had a tablet that was connected to the UNGAR MMXX where it could advise him what moves to make. Out of sight from the players but visible by the audience was a huge TV screen that showed the community cards that both players could use to complete their hand, but again, not their individual hidden cards until the hand was over. Both on the Tomas's tablet as well as the big screen above the dealer, UNGAR MMXX displayed all the optimal moves that Tomas should take, which were then meant to be executed. With each decision the computer suggested, it gave a confidence level, along with the degree of accuracy it calculated about each play. For instance, when first to act, an output might suggest that the optimal play would be to bet half the pot 60% of the time, bet the size of the pot 30% of the time, and check 10% of the time. Another example might be when faced with a decision to fold, call or raise, an output might be that the right decision in this instance would be to call 70% of the time, raise the size of the pot 15% of the time, go all-in 14% of the time and fold 1% of the time. If faced with an all-in decision where the only options were call or fold, UNGAR MMXX could suggest that calling would be the correct play x% of the time, depending on its own holdings and the range of holdings for its opponents based on game theory as well as player-specific patterns observed throughout the match. Tomas would then take the decision with the highest confidence level, as he placed all his confidence in the computer's decision-making process.

As we were getting closer to the start, I started feeling the tension, as well as started to hypothesize how this could end. The most likely outcome was clearly going to be a win by UNGAR MMXX and PiMS. What would that do to Johnny's legacy? What would that do to the outlook for humanity and its ability to compete with machines taking jobs? Did Johnny even care, knowing that he was at worst going to walk away with a quarter of a million dollars to which he could then go at sit at a table with Doyle to try to avenge an old loss from 1957? His history suggests he was a man always seeking action, so perhaps he didn't place any grand importance on the match. Hypothetically speaking, if Johnny was to win, how would that happen? Would it be with some miracle one-outer on the River with his final card, like famous stories of Nick the Greek or Lancey Howard? Surely Johnny was not going to participate in something that was more likely to occur in his earlier years as a road gambler, like having the game hijacked by armed robbers, or perhaps more appropriate in the modern setting, arranging for someone to accidentally kick over the power cord to his unsuspecting adversary? While I was still uncertain to the exact reason he was brought back, those endings would not have been consistent with Anyone's grander plan of reincarnating this legend to the game.

After an elaborate set of introductions by some of the senior members of PiMS as well as some ratings-inspiring talk by the ESPN announcers, the match was finally underway. As soon as the first cards were dealt,

Johnny appeared very calm and very comfortable. He had been here before, in big games in what may have been seemingly intense situations to others, but none of that showed on his face. He was back at home at the poker table.

Probably similar to the likely mundane first days of that historic heads-up session with Nick the Greek, Johnny's first few episodes in this televised program (two-hour sessions from 9:00-11:00 PM on ESPN) had him playing a pretty unexciting role, with the match going exactly as anyone familiar with the modern game of poker would have expected. Johnny was no mathematician. Nor did his knowledge of Morse Code help him decipher any deep meaning from the computer's confidence levels. He dropped out of school prior to starting the third grade, and despite his great card sense and general math sense (such as never drawing to an Inside Straight unless the pot odds suggested otherwise), made several tiny errors in his calling, folding, betting and raising frequencies that slowly chipped away at his tournament stack of chips. It didn't appear as if Johnny was giving away any information from his facial expressions. While it has been observed that even top professionals have tells that give away the strength of their hand, I wasn't surprised to see, at least to my amateur eyes, no clear tells with Johnny. He had played poker for so long; did any set of cards, good or bad, or any decision, easy or difficult, leave him even feeling happy or sad, let alone expressing it? Whether he won or lost, his expressions showed the face of a man doing what he was meant to be doing, exerting the minimal effort needed to excel.

He successfully bluffed the machine a few times, but this was to be expected, as calling every possible bluff is a losing strategy for any poker player, whether made of silicon or flesh. Johnny did suggest a few side bets, as remember, he was allowed to name the stakes. With them, he would suggest to Tomas that in addition to tournament chips, he would suggest a bet (of real cash) on the hand. If he won the best, he won the cash, if he lost, Tomas returned the winnings to PiMS's balance. Johnny won more of those than he lost; for instance, he won a few thousand dollars in one hand where UNGAR MMXX dictated that it was fairly unlikely that Johnny held a Queen and a Jack when the computer held another Jack and a board of Ten-Nine-Eight-Seven-Six, giving the computer the Straight but Johnny a higher Straight. The computer's output suggested "just" a 55% confidence interval that calling Johnny's bet was the correct play, so Tomas did it, then nonchalantly shrugged his shoulders, as again, no poker player alive, dead or otherwise, always makes the right decision. This was basically a coin flip, and Tomas had no issues acting where the computer gave even the slightest preference for one play over another. Despite some of these smaller wins for Johnny that were often a few thousand dollars, there was no way that he was going to make up the difference between the payouts of first and second place at the current rate that he was bleeding tournament chips.

The outcome of the event, with the slow drip going against Johnny's fortune, seemed pretty close to being decided. Machine was not only better than man at calculating pots odds and bet sizes, using Game Theory to deduce raising frequencies and such, but also better at "learning," where it analysed its opponent's tendencies and then came up ways to exploit them. Surely even an elementary school drop-out like Johnny must have realized this prior, or at least now, during the match? If he did, his face didn't show it, keeping the same stoic poker face from the initiation of the match to the point we're at now. Johnny once said that "in an otherwise even contest, the man with the best concentration will almost always win." Johnny was concentrating. And for the sixty-three-year-old looking Grand Old Man, he didn't look tired or run down like he later looked in life. Johnny was clearly paying attention to what the computer was doing and how his human counterpart was confidently obeying his machine-master's every command.

Johnny's face didn't change, nor did those alligator eyes lose their focus, even as it was clear to all that the human was at the clear disadvantage.

Most heads-up matches don't take that long. PiMS clearly had an interest in not only making this a fair event but also one that would last at least three episodes, so both players were given an ample amount of starting chips so that neither would be devastated by any single big pot and be able to deal with the natural variance of the game. If they were given one chip each and asked to ante that chip before getting their cards, the match would come down to luck. If they were given infinite chips, the winner would always be the best player. While not infinite, enough chips were given so that after six hours of play (or three episodes), a winner would be crowned and no disputes would be made to the legitimacy of the event's structure.

At the start of the third episode, where it was clear to many that this might be the final episode of the series, the tension of the event started to subside. Several PiMS executives had brought in their family members to attend. Tomas's wife and two young children attended on the final day as well, while others who had attended the initial games were replaced by new viewers who although missed the opening excitement, would at least be there to witness how the event ended. Sitting in socially-distanced seating, the crowd stretched pretty far back from where the main table was, and after an early break in the action, I partook in the ritual typically reserved for breaks in any large poker tournament, namely the fast-walk to the restroom before it reaches its capacity and the waiting-line extends beyond the entrance. On the way back, in scanning those already in their seats, I was fairly certain that I had passed several of Johnny's grandchildren and great grandchildren. I had only seen a few pictures of them in doing my research on Facebook, but given that a few of my vague recollections of their faces all seemed to be sitting in the same area, I felt fairly certain that this was his family. As he hadn't made any mention of them to me, I wondered if he even knew they were there.

Two huge checks were placed near the poker table, with the names to be filled in at the conclusion. While many clearly took note of this symbolic display, more could be seen distracted on their phones than focusing in on the final moments of yet another chapter of the man versus machine story that had been told a countless amount of times already over the last hundred or so years. Disney's adaptation of the story of the mythical Paul Bunyan comes to mind as an early legend of one of these such losses. Mister Bunyan couldn't beat the machines at cutting down and logging timber, even with the help of his pet, Babe the Blue Ox. Garry Kasparov and Ken Jennings didn't fare much better in their respective games involving more brain than brawn. It appeared Johnny Moss was about to join that list of fallen legends.

Johnny had not been too talkative to Tomas during much of the match, as other than suggesting a few side bets, his calls, raises and folds typically just involved the minimal expulsion of energy in either tossing in chips or throwing away losing cards. Perhaps the clear change of the game's mood and near conclusion nudged him to loosen up.

"You have a nice family there, son. How many years you been married?"

"I just reached twelve, thanks Johnny. I've been happily married for twelve years," motioning to the general area in the crowd where his wife was seated.

With a glance to the crowd, Johnny then added "And are those your two boys in the audience with her?"

"Yes, the oldest is eleven and the youngest is nine. I couldn't have asked for better sons."

"Oh, that's nice. Wife, boys, I'll bet PiMS keeps you well paid too, right?"

"Uh, yeah, they do. We're comfortable."

"I must say, I always had a problem holdin' on to money" Johnny admitted. "I always let my wife, Virgie, manage the important finances of house and things, as while I could earn it quick, I was also known to lose it even quicker. I know this is a personal question, but I have to ask, as your life seems like an enviable one." With that, he started to almost whisper, leaning in a little more, clearly about to pay attention to the response he was going to get. "Just between us, and not for the television audience, how much is someone like you worth?"

"Ha, well, thanks for the compliment, Johnny. I've been a saver my while life, not quite living the gambling lifestyle you had. With both my wife and I having pretty good salaries, combined with living below our incomes and investing in low-fee ETF's mirroring the S&P500, we're worth about four million dollars. Oh, plus the house. And that's also not counting the limited-edition Audi R8. We don't usually spend that much on vehicles, but my wife has really been wanting something to show off to her friends, and Christmas was coming up, so I splurged..."

Watching Johnny watching Tomas as he was explaining his riches was pretty intense to anyone who is at all adept in reading people, as he seemed to be studying him, taking in more than just the words of his opponent but clearly noticing his facial expressions, hand movements, even breathing patterns. After he apparently heard enough, Johnny cut him off, clearly no longer interested in the small talk and getting to know the softer-side of the flesh and blood that was representing his adversary sitting in the other chair. About as unemotionally as it could have been said, he replied "You've done well for yourself, Tomas. Fine job, with your finances and family." Then, sensing his purpose for being here might be close to being realized, noted "Should we get back to the game now?"

The game continued as did the slow drip of Johnny's chips from his side of the table to the other. The methodical slicing away at his stack by UNGAR MMXX was akin to a surgeon replacing a butcher at the local meat shop; instead of using a cleaver to chop off larger portions of the red meat, a scalpel was used to shave off nearly transparent layers, though layers nonetheless. While we all trusted that UNGAR MMXX didn't know Johnny's hole cards, it was clear that it was just making more correct plays than Johnny, and despite Johnny making some adjustments as well, his were not as accurate as the computer's. It was at this realization for me that I noticed what I thought was the Moss family getting up as a group and exiting the room. Again, I'm not sure Johnny noticed them.

A short while later, *the* hand finally happened. Johnny was holding the Ace-Ten off-suit, which coincidentally, was the hand that was named "The Johnny Moss" in Doyle Brunson's originally titled *How I Made Over $1,000,000 Playing Poker*. The Ace was of

Spades, the "prettiest card in the deck," as World Series of Poker commentator Norman Chad had proclaimed it. The Ten was a Diamond. Johnny was first to act and limped in to complete the minimum bet so that he could continue in the hand. Johnny had been fairly consistent in how he played his hands containing an Ace up to this point; he had raised all of his suited Aces when he was first to act and employed a mixed strategy of limping or betting with unsuited Aces. After his action, the computer suggested a check, to which Tomas agreed. With a rarely dangerous Seven-Three-Deuce on Flop, the computer suggested a check. But wait, all the cards on the Flop were Spades. This gave Johnny a draw to the best possible Flush, but at this point, he still only had Ace High. If the hand ended now and the computer held any Seven, Three, Deuce, any Pocket Pair, any Ace-King, Ace-Queen, Ace-Jack, or two Spades, Johnny would lose. With a draw to the best hand, or nuts, Johnny bet half the size of the pot of tournament chips, to which UNGAR MMXX suggested a raise. Tomas accepted the suggestion, as he always did, to which Johnny then called. The Turn was the Eight of Hearts. The computer checked again (accepted by Tomas), Johnny again bet half the pot, with the UNGAR MMXX again suggesting a check-raise (accepted by Tomas), to which Johnny again called, still with just Ace High. The River was the Jack of Diamonds. Again, the computer suggested a check, and again Johnny bet half the pot, and as a rarely seen play, UNGAR MMXX suggested its third check-raise. Facing a triple check-raise, all poker players know that Johnny's showdown value if he calls is next to nothing, as the computer has shown enormous strength by making this play, screaming out to even the most novice of players that it has a really big holding. Even weak hands, like any holding carrying a Deuce, Three, Seven, Eight or Jack gives the computer a Pair. A Nine-Ten now gives the computer a Straight. The Ace-King, Ace-Queen and Ace-Jack are still ahead of Johnny, as well as the numerous combinations of Flopped Flushes that are highly possible given the way the computer played the hand if it held two Spades. King of Spades – Queen of Spades would have been a very reasonable hand to put UNGAR MMXX on, which of course beats Johnny's busted Flush Draw.

So where did that leave our hero? Before we go there, it's worth reminding everyone of the different levels of poker thinking. Level One is when you know what you have. You can see your cards and you know their relative strength given the community cards that both you and your opponent can use. If you have Queen-Three and the board is Three-Three-Three-Seven-Nine, you have Four of a Kind. That's Level One. Level Two is where you start thinking about what your opponent has. Once you get comfortable with this level, you can start playing beyond your own cards. If you're pretty sure your opponent has Queen-Jack based on him just check/calling a bet on a Flop of Ten of Hearts, Nine of Hearts, Three of Spades (which he might do with the exact two cards he has, giving him the Nut

Straight Draw), followed by him just checking/calling the Turn of the Deuce of Clubs, followed by him checking the Ace of Diamonds, you can then bet your busted Flush Draw of Five of Hearts / Six of Hearts, because you know he can't call with just Queen High. That's Level Two. Level Three is where you start thinking about what your opponent thinks *you* have. If after every time you have ever check-raised your opponent, you show him a strong hand, you can occasionally then start doing that as a bluff, as you will think that they will think that you're strong. That's Level Three. Level Four and higher get into the "what do you think they think you think..." thought process, and as you can imagine, gets a bit tougher.

So what was Johnny thinking when the computer check-raised him three times on a Three-Flush board? Johnny of course wasn't smart enough to know all the calculations that the computer was doing which told it that check-raising was the best possible play, though what he was 100% certain of was that he knew that UNGAR MMXX knew that it did not have the best possible hand, given that Johnny held the Ace of Spades, which was a Blocker to the best hand. For all UNGAR MMXX knew, Johnny possessed the Ace of Spades along with one of the other Spades that was not on the board (or in its digital hands). He also knew that UNGAR MMXX knew that he had always raised with his suited aces, which he had not done this hand. Given that, the triple check-raise didn't shock him, but he knew the computer wouldn't be certain whether or not its clearly-strong hand was best.

"Well this is shaping up to be a pretty interestin' hand" said Johnny. His own mental calculator was clearly working, weighting several variables of his own, though likely not the binary zeros and ones that his opponent was doing at a much faster rate. With his pondering, the game had paused momentarily, likely less than a minute, though it seemed much longer than that. Eventually the silence broke when Johnny stated "I think I'd like to raise the stakes on this one."

"Whatever you say, Johnny. What would you like to play for this time?"

"Well, to start, I'd like to raise some tournament chips by doublin' that last bet. But then in addition, I'd like to play this pot for four million dollars in cash."

That was said just loud enough so that the audience, who had clearly been starting to tune out, came back with a combined gasp. That bet was far outside the other bets of a few thousand dollars that Johnny had made up to that point.

"Well that's a pretty big bet, Johnny." replied Tomas. "If I can indeed secure that amount of money, I assume you can show proof that you're good for it if you lose?"

"Oh, I'm most definitely good for it. Despite being dead for a long time now, my reputation has stayed around long enough that I was able to secure enough backin' for any bet I was going to make on this show. I can have my backers call into a telephone number on the screen and wire the money into a holdin' account as soon as your team sets that up, if you'd like?"

Tomas was taken aback by this somewhat unexpected turn of events, though tried putting on his own best poker face to not show any weakness on either his own part or the part of the company he was representing.

"Oh, ok, that's fine, Johnny. But just to make it clear to you – and our now-engaged studio audience – that even if you bet the four million dollars and the computer suggests a fold, you wouldn't actually win four million dollars, but you would just win the tournament chips currently in the pot, which would still leave you substantially far behind in the overall tournament. And of course you would get the four million dollars of your own money back."

"I'm aware of that."

"Ok then, let's take a commercial break here then and go through the formalities of me asking my superiors at PiMS if we can secure the four million dollars for you *just in case* the computer decides we should call your bet."

"Oh, checking with PiMS won't be necessary, Tomas." Johnny said this without hesitation and somewhat matter-of-factly. He spoke with a lack of emotion that made it clear to poker players watching that his intentions were unreadable by human opponents. He also spoke in a volume that was clearly not just meant for Tomas but instead just loud enough that the studio audience could clearly hear his every word. "As one of the provisions of this game that we agreed to in writin' was that I would be able to name the stakes, I'm callin' it out that I'm raisin' this pot four million dollars of *my* money against four million dollars of *your* money, Tomas. Oh, and that new car as well."

The crowd gasped again but then went completely silent. The proverbial pin drop was clearly heard. Tomas's face almost immediately lost all color, as he clearly understood what Johnny had said. UNGAR MMXX also understood almost as quickly given its voice-activation software, outputting the certainty that calling the four-million-dollar bet was the correct decision at 86%. This was by far the most "confident" that the computer had been in any of its decisions.

Poker is a game of incomplete information. Any poker player, whether making its decisions based on bits or brains, know that as long as the opponent conceals his or her cards, there's no real certainty in any decision, but just an educated guess or inference about the unknown in that opponent's hands. For reference, holding the best starting hand in Texas Hold Em (a Pair of Aces) versus the second-best hand (Pocket Kings) yields the Aces an 80% favorite to win over the Kings. All poker players would jump at being put in a position with such favorable odds at their local game.

But this was not their local game. Sure, there were a few "sure bets" in poker, such as when you have the "unbreakable nuts," which is a hand that can't be beat no matter what your opponent holds or what cards may appear later. But in poker, as in life for that matter, sure bets are few and far between.

Johnny, still stone-faced, reiterated the bet, adding in the recent but obvious new piece of information. "This computer of yours suggests that you make the call, Tomas. Are you goin' to make the call?"

Before Tomas could take another breath, a voice from the studio audience burst out, and was getting louder and louder as it approached the table and its audio equipment.

"Tommy, don't you *dare* lose our fortune to that man! And don't you dare lose my new car that you just bought me to him either!"

Of course this turn of events seemed unexpected to everyone, especially Mister Christopher, who was just yelled at publicly in front of a live studio audience and an entire nation watching on ESPN by Misses Christopher. Though now having completed one breath, he did what the majority of husbands would do, turning away from Johnny and giving his newly socially-undistant wife his undivided attention.

"Calm down, dear" were the first words out of his mouth, though as soon as he uttered them, he realized that they were a mistake, as that is never an appropriate response to a loving partner in any circumstance. And they were especially bad words as they were more reflected back at himself, as he clearly was not calm during this unexpected turn of events. "The computer is suggesting that there's a very strong likelihood that we would win the bet."

Tomas's wife, clearly not illiterate in third grade math, rebutted quickly. "The way I'm reading those numbers is that the computer 'thinks' that 14% of the time, we're going broke. Is that correct?"

This time a huge bucket of proverbial pins was dropped from the ceiling at the Rio, as ESPN's audio equipment clearly picked up the panicked pace and deeper breathings of Tomas's recycling of oxygen.

"Well, yeah, sort of..." were the first uneasy words out of Tomas's mouth, while it was clear that his wife, normally of a slightly bronzed skin color was quickly transforming into one with a hue closer to the final card dealt in this big hand, the red Jack of Diamonds.

Tomas's wife did not let him complete the thought, though it was clear to many that Tomas may not have had a response worth uttering. She burst out with what almost seemed like a scripted line of "If you lose our fortune, I'm filing for a divorce immediately. And you won't be seeing the kids again, either."

To the untrained eye, this almost appeared to be a scene from The Jerry Springer Show, with a fuming partner ready to explode, though this time the fury wasn't in response to a cheating partner but instead

one that might...just might...make a really, really bad

decision. But wait, the computer. UNGAR MMXX, with

its facial coding software, game theory background and

exploitative observations, yielded an 86% certainty that

calling the bet would be correct. Previous calculations

were never that high unless of course it was certain

that it held the best hand. This seemed to be the

moment he was actually waiting for prior to the match,

where he would show the world how powerful his

computer was, adding yet another notch in PiMS's and

AI's belt of powerful human victims it had left in the

dust.

So what was going on here? The wise thing to do

would be to take a deep breath and assess the

situation. Taking a deep breath always helps.

Sometimes a few breaths is even better. Surely Johnny

clearly knew that a situation like this would come up

sometime in the match; why else would he add in the

prerequisite of naming the stakes and all that small

talk of assessing his net worth to come up with the bet size of four million dollars? If Johnny was aware of this ahead of time, perhaps this would be the perfect time to make a big bluff just like this, knowing how difficult it would be to call. On the other hand, what if Johnny was playing his game against the computer, knowing he couldn't beat it in the long run to win the one million dollars for first place but instead set up this one hand perfectly so that losing the one million dollars wouldn't even matter if he was to win the four million dollars for this hand and the two hundred fifty thousand for second place? Oh, and he would also get the new Audi for his getaway car after launching and completing this perfectly legal and even agreed-upon-by-PiMS heist.

A few more breaths. Sure, a notch in PiMS's belt would be nice. He would likely get a raise for that. Would the additional four million dollars for winning the bet change his life for the better? Losing it sure would stink. And oh yeah, he was happily married with two kids, so losing them wouldn't be a desirable outcome. What if he called and actually won? Would his wife be happy that he was willing to "gamble" their family for a "mere" doubling of their already-comfortable net worth? Tomas was a smart man and one who made good thought-out decisions his whole life. He started to think he was outside of his element with such a decision placed upon him, even after carefully thinking through all the variables. Despite the potential reward, the personal risk of ruin seemed to be pushing him toward a decision that should have been an easy one.

"I'm going to decline the computer's suggestion, Johnny," Tomas said, proudly, though with a huge exhale. "With my fold, you'll win the tournament chips already in the pot and nothing else, and we can go on to the next hand."

His words came out almost too fluidly, as if he didn't quite grasp what he was saying. There was some immediate rumbling in the audience and a sense of uncertainty of what just happened, though Johnny didn't hesitate to respond himself.

"Well I guess that means I won the match and the one million dollars, doesn't it, Tomas?"

A bit confused but also angry, Tomas responded quickly, again not fully thinking through his response. "No!" was his shouted reply that surprised himself and the audience. "The computer was clearly beating you prior to your four million dollar shenanigans and it will continue to beat you if we keep playing. So let's keep playing!"

After this final shout, the crowd went silent again, this time waiting for Johnny's response. Johnny had played every hand up to this point with a calm and collected demeanor, so no one was sure how this formerly gun-carrying Texan road gambler would react to a leader-of-engineers aggressively shouting at him.

Johnny absorbed Tomas's remarks, took a breath himself, and with an almost even-calmer-than-normal tone, though with extreme gravitas, replied "Son, I had thought this was a contest between man and machine. If you're not gonna accept the computer's recommendation on what was clearly the most difficult decision of the match, I think you're gonna to find it a hard case to defend that the computer should be the winner."

Chapter 9 :

Celebration and Post Mortem

A few hours later, after the audience had dispersed, the cameras taken down and UNGAR MMXX unplugged and removed from the Rio, I found Johnny at a roulette table in the main casino, making much larger bets than I would have thought him comfortable.

"Mister Moss, you're betting amounts like money is going out of style," I bellowed.

"Found money is better to bet than money you worked for," he snickered back.

"So how'd you do that back there? I'm not sure there has ever been a poker audience or poker opponent so set in awe after what they just witnessed. The look on Tomas's face when you made that final statement was like a frying pan just hitting him in the face. He seemed like he was never going to speak again."

Johnny responded after the numbers he had played, a Two and a Nineteen, representing his daughter Eleoweese's birthday, didn't turn up, with the spinning ball's resting place on the Black Ten instead.

"Poor sucker never had a chance. They never do. I've played against scientific players before and they never really win."

"But Mister Moss, the computer was beating you the entire match. Slowly but surely it was clear to everyone that it was making slightly better decisions than you the whole tournament. If it was just you versus the computer, you lose, right?"

"I never signed up to play against a computer," he chuckled, while placing a bet on the Five and Eight, representing the date he won the inaugural World Series of Poker Main Event. "I agreed to play against a man with a calculator. Despite my speech at the end there, the nice part was that Tomas just didn't know it until it was too late."

Now it was I that was speechless. Wow. Had he played us all the whole time? Or was this the point; that there was no such thing as a "man versus machine" match without man's approval? Sure, ATM's do it all the time, as no one at the bank is signing off on each machine's handing-over of hundreds of dollars after those personally meaningful numbers are entered into its interface. But if the executives at JPMorgan Chase Bank realized that their ATM's were spitting out one twenty-dollar bill too many in every transaction, the plug is going to be pulled really quickly until it is reprogrammed.

I like to define "genius" as someone who sees things that others cannot. In hindsight, everything that Johnny did made perfect sense, but how was it that no one else was aware? None of us found it overly suspicious that Johnny had just two stipulations to the contract, as we couldn't see what advantage that gave him. And we all took him for granted, as an old man, even in rebirth probably still past his prime, with surely not with enough brainpower to outclass the computational power of the machine. With literally nothing to lose (as remember, he didn't even have to pay his entry into the tournament), we thought that PiMS had everything to gain. With it quite the opposite, most of us were wrong, which says something about Johnny.

"So what are you going to do with one million dollars? There's no doubt that a man in your situation has better things to do with a million dollars than play the numbers on a game of chance."

"Oh, I earned more than a million dollars on that game."

As my eyes gave him a new stare with eyebrows now raised, I anticipated what I was sure would be an even bigger surprise ending to this story, to which he started into it pretty quickly.

"That Phil Ivey is one cool character. Despite me growin' up when segregation was not only legal but it was taught that blacks and whites ain't equal, it don't take a genius to figure that none athat is true once you get to know someone. As soon as I met him I know there was somethin' special 'bout him just by the way he looked at me. He knew who I was and he was checkin' me out as if he might pick up somethin' about me just by my mannerisms. Once I formally introduced myself, we got to talkin' straight away."

"I'm sure the poker community would have loved to have been a fly on that wall! With two luminaries of the game talking poker..."

Johnny interrupted as soon as he heard my mistake. "Oh we didn't talk poker. We got on a golf course, as we both have the same likin' for the game and gamblin' on it. The name of the game is winnin' the game. Once I told him about this PiMS game and what the game was and that I was goin' to win it, he had an idea, how should I put it, to compound my winnings."

"Oh boy. Do tell?"

"Of course. Remember when I told Tomas that based on my reputation, I was good for the money needed for the side bet? Well, that was sorta true. I did find backers though it was for a lot more money than that, so I took the money upfront. What did I do with the money? Well, I never heard of this back in my day, but I invested a rather large sum into 'shortin' PiMS, as I knew their stock would fall after losin' to me. And, well, what do you know, that bet paid off quite handsomely as well. I owe Phil Ivey a 'thank you, partna' for that suggestion."

Not only was I speechless after hearing this new story but my jaw had dropped to a level I wasn't sure it could. Not only had Johnny played the game masterfully, but in knowing he was going to win the game, increased his total profit from the win by anticipating what Wall Street traders were going to do the next day based on the outcome.

Beyond genius. While clearly smart, did Johnny go beyond an acceptable form of competition and participate in a contest that wasn't quite on the up and up? Legendary gamblers like Amarillo Slim Preston and Titanic Thompson tricked opponents into thinking they were getting a square deal on wagers when often they weren't. Sometimes they dealt fairly, while of course hiding important information about a proposition, though sometimes they devised schemes so elaborate that no one could possibly look at them after the fact and believe they were attempting to make bets that their opponents had any chance of winning. What is the difference between a con and a fair contest? I won't go into a dissertation on the moral or legal definitions of cheating, but I don't think this episode fell into that category. Perhaps to simplify it, in a con, there is no question as to the outcome of the engagement, where in a fair contest, there is.

When I could put together a few words after hearing about this double-bonus he received for the win, these came out. "Was there ever any doubt about this plan?"

He looked a little older as he responded, more like the grandfatherly figure that an unassuming onlooker would have guessed about his identity versus the cold-blooded gambler that he was. "Sure, there was a little doubt. There's always a little doubt. There are no certainties in life, and certainly not in poker. I was the best player for a very long time but I didn't win every tournament I entered or leave every cash game a winner. But more times than not luck stays on the side of the person who works hardest at his craft, payin' attention to what he was doin', being mindful of each moment. When you're in the game, and I mean really in the game, it's almost hard to miss opportunities that you can profit from. And when I say 'in the game,' I mean any game you're in."

Poker historian Johnny Hughes once wrote that Doyle Brunson was quoted as saying that Johnny was more fearless, more dedicated and more consumed by poker than anyone he had ever known. That dedication was clear in this story we just witnessed.

"The way that contest was set up, it could have finished where neither of us emerged a notable winner. If the computer won, well, it was supposed to win, and that's not much of a contest. It wins first place and I get a nice consolation prize, with no investment on my part. But I reckoned if there was a chance of real winnin' to be done, which I figured there was, well, it might as well have been me that did it. That's important. Lookin' for opportunities where others don't see them. And that goes versus these computers too. Sure, you can lose to them if you want, in any walk of life. Though if you're wise, you can outsmart the brainless and soulless machines by tryin' to really understand the game you're playin'."

Was this the message he was brought back to give us? In today's world with so much automation or algorithms apparently sucking the humanity out of us, perhaps many were looking at the game all wrong. Even Garry Kasparov, who had perhaps the most famous loss to a machine in human history, later admitted that losing (chess) to the machine was eventually inevitable, with Deep Blue's victory against him not the key takeaway. He argued that we humans might as well be machines ourselves if we lose our ability to dream big and search for greater purpose, often with the help of machine's strengths to help take us further. Perhaps the most iconic combination of man with machine was in how computers helped man achieve the culmination of all those dreams of landing on the moon. The computer never had that dream and wasn't about to do it by itself. Whether something as grand as landing on the moon or as trivial as winning a game of cards, or anything in between, truly understanding our goals shouldn't be stopped by machines, only helped.

"Johnny Moss, I was a fan of yours before meeting you in person, but now I'm even more impressed. You really seem to have a grasp on some of the bigger-picture issues that took place at this game. The end result for you seems to have been a lot of money. So, I'll ask again, what are you going to do with all of it?"

Johnny had just won one of the most noteworthy competitions in history, though sadness now gleamed over his face, which almost seemed like it aged him a few years in the past few seconds. "Ah, money. I was never really good at handlin' money. I could win it better than most, but I couldn't hold on to it. There's stories about how I lost a lot on rollin' dice and bettin' horses, and I suppose most of them are true. There was that one story where I told Virgie to buy a house one day, then after a huge loss, told her the next day she better not go buy that house anymore. I later made sure she held my money. She bought some apartments with it that I think my great-grandkids still own today, so that always kept us financially sound. Later on the Binion's helped me out a bit, givin' me just enough for what I needed to get by on, as I stayed up in Las Vegas for a while, as that's where the action was. But I can't handle money, and perhaps worse, I realized early on that I may notta been the best at dealin' with family either."

I didn't want to probe too much on that topic. Little was written about Johnny's relationship with his wife. He was often seen at the casino while his wife was in an assisted living facility. The biography that was published under his name didn't note the joy that might have been associated with a first-born and no record exists of a strong relationship with his daughter or grandchildren. I had tried reaching out to one of his grandsons, who was now an old man himself, and his wife was kind enough to write me a short note back.

She shared a few facts with me, that Johnny was once on a gameshow called "To Tell The Truth" (which I believed, but couldn't verify) and on The Merv Griffin Show (which I verified, though sadly couldn't find a copy of the episode). One line from her note to me seemed to validate everything else I had learned about the man, in that she respectively noted that the only thing he wanted to do was play poker. In doing a little more research on the family I found the obituary for his daughter, Eleoweese, who had three sons and lived to the old age of eighty-six, passing away in 2013 in Odessa, Texas. Her obituary noted something I couldn't find regarding Johnny, in that she seemed to live a very happy life and was very kind to others, and in retirement, was noted to be enjoying her time with her kids, grandkids and great-grandkids. Despite his greatness, Johnny's glory in his game and lifestyle of choice highlighted the endless possibilities of success when hard work is combined with concentration. At the same time, such a singular focus on any undertaking seemed to make it very clear that we can't be everything, underscoring the frailty of the human condition. Perhaps this was the message that we should be taking away; that despite our quest for greatness, whether versus man or machine, life may not be worth going through – once or again – if the relationships we keep are not valued even more than the victories we seek.

"Some folks say that if they had a chance to do it all over again they would change a few things while others say they wouldn't change a thing. If you wanna change somethin' about yourself, great, get to it. What I've realized for me is that this is who I am and I've got no interest in changin' that."

Fair enough. He is Johnny Moss, perhaps the greatest poker player of all time. I am an avid poker player and storyteller and just glad we all got to experience this one last narrative together, hopefully taking away a few lessons from his final tale.

Johnny Moss and Ed Chiaramonte,

Binion's Gambling Hall, Las Vegas, NV, 2018.

Afterward :

Ramblings on the GOAT

Chapter 10 :

The Greatest Of All Time and Mount Rushmore

With Johnny Moss's history now complete, this last chapter is an attempt to provide a framework for thinking about the question of who is the greatest poker player of all time. If singularity is tough, perhaps the easier and lately more fashionable way to ask a similar question is "Who should be on the Mount Rushmore of Poker?" With that, I will attempt to provide not only the variables to consider when trying to make this argument about poker players, but one that can be used in debating the greatest of all time at anything.

The question of course is a silly one. "Greatest" is a subjective term and opinions will undoubtably vary. "Poker player" is also a questionable term. "All Time" warrants a definition. Despite the subjectivity and vagueness around even the terms of the question, I would like to lay out a framework for the discussion. You may disagree with the framework and of course disagree with the concluding Mount Rushmore, though as per the introduction to this paragraph, it's all subjective. Even with subjectivity though, I think there's value in attempting to set up a framework that can be used as the blueprint for determining "greatest" at anything. Is there value in this exercise? I think yes; if greatness is your goal, it seems logical to try to define it so that you have something specific to aim for. Let's start by trying to define some of the terms.

First, let's start trying to define "poker." Perhaps simply, we know it's a game played with cards that have different values when combined with other cards that involves wagering. There are many *ways* to play a poker game. There is a huge difference between the play in *cash games*, where players risk money on each hand they play versus *tournaments*, where there is no money to lose once the entry (or entries for rebuy tournaments) are paid. In the "modern" era, there are still *live* games (that can be played anywhere from casinos in Monte Carlo to the basements of a home in Easton, Connecticut) as well as *online* games (where that is legal). There are also different *variants* of poker, such as No Limit Texas Hold Em, Pot Limit Omaha High Low Eight or Better, or Deuce to Seven Triple Draw. Even more recently, there are distinctions based on the *amount of the buy-in*, where some players perform much better versus lower buy-in fields of non-professionals while others excel even at the super high-roller stakes versus the game's elite. Given the different ways to play and variants of the game, it is not a novel thought that when trying to define the greatest "poker player" that the term should be used to describe someone who plays many of these ways and variants well. If they do not, a qualifier would be added to "poker player," such as describing someone as "she's a good <No Limit> <Texas Hold Em> <Tournament> 'poker player'" versus just being described as a great "poker player." The best No Limit Texas Hold Em tournament player may barely know the rules of some other poker games, given their clear focus on mastery of just one game, and it would likely not be an insult if someone were awarded the title of "Best No Limit Texas Hold Em tournament player in non High-Roller events," which might go to someone like Stu Ungar or Phil Hellmuth. But it seems somewhat self-evident that the Greatest Poker Player without any qualifiers should play all the ways/variants well.

Another point we'll want to define is "all time," as well as "time." Let's start with the easier of those which is "time." Let's start outside of poker for a comparison point, and look at the running back position in the National Football League. This was always my favorite to watch growing up, with the player I liked the most being Barry Sanders. In terms of just running the ball, it was amazing the things he was able to do on the football field. If we think strictly of what the running back is asked to do, "running" might be the purest requirement. Yes, they are expected to catch the occasional pass or block for the quarterback, but for now let's ask who the greatest "runner" in the running back position was in the history of football. There's a simple statistic for this, which is the number of yards a runner gets when handed the football, or "yards per carry." Keeping to this simple approach, Jim Brown averaged 5.2 yards per carry. There are a lot of other statistics and stories that might convince you that Jim Brown was not only the greatest running back of all time but the greatest football player of all time. Needless to say, Jim Brown was an all-time great running back. Barry Sanders averaged 5.0 yards per carry, which was also amazing, to go with other statistically great numbers and one of the best highlight reels of footage of any runner. Despite both leaving the game early in their careers, both played long enough to rank among the best at the all-time rankings of *total* yards as well as yards per carry.

So here we have two players, both with long careers, not only piling up statistics due to their longevity but also great statistics in the smallest of intervals, per just an average single carry. There is one running back who may have been more dominant – and perhaps more popular – than either of them, though given the (unfortunate) shortness of his career, is rarely even given a footnote in any Greatest Of All Time debate. Bo Jackson averaged 5.4 yards per carry over four seasons. While there is no formal definition of a "long" career, his amazing statistics were clearly not performed long enough for Hall of Fame voters to place his career among the profession's best, nor is he seriously considered when experts or casual fans talk about the all-time great runners. With respect to poker, Doyle Brunson has answered the question of "Who are the best players today?" with the answer of "Ask me again in 30-40 years and I'll tell you." Poker's Hall of Fame has as one of its requirements that members "stood the test of time." Clearly this suggests that it takes more than a big-tournament win (even if that one win puts you at the all-time tournament earnings leader, as it did for Antonio Esfandiari when he won the inaugural one million dollar buy-in The Big One for One Drop event for a first place prize of $18,346,673 in 2012) or a good week at the Las Vegas cash tables to appoint a great poker player. It seems an easy point to make that longevity is a variable in determining qualification into the "all time" greatest debate.

In thinking about poker players, the aspect of "time" (as a comparative point), or more specifically, age, gets more interesting. An accomplished poker like Phil Ivey fits all the qualifications of a great poker player (with more on him later), with his formal career spanning from his twenty-first birthday until today (he is currently forty-three years old at the time of this writing). How would we compare him to Johnny Moss, who not only had a great poker career from his youth until age forty-three, but also a great career from forty-three until age sixty-three, and then at that youthful age, just started his World Series of Poker career, amassing nine World Series of Poker bracelets up until his eighty-first birthday? With the World Series of Poker and tournament poker starting late in Johnny Moss's career, what would his resume look like if it had started at his twenty-first birthday? Yes, the smaller fields of earlier years had a positive impact on his tournament wins, though whether it was defeating the handful of other contestants willing to sit down with him in 1970 for his first win or the 193 he had to outlast to win his last in 1988, neither the number of competitors nor his age seemed to hold back his performance. Will the best players of today be able to compete when they are more senior? While Phil Ivey's career of over twenty years is clearly one of the best during his "mental prime," and I am clearly not trying to call him the Bo Jackson of Poker, how should we put any shorter career into perspective when Johnny Moss was not only a top player during an identical age span, but also a top player when increased age began wearing on his mental acuity and physical ability to play for the long hours required for the profession?

One can begin to tease out aspects of time to make comparisons easier, though they too aren't perfect. Going back to football, if we want to compare Bo Jackson to Jim Brown or Barry Sanders *in their best years*, we can pick their best four years and compare. Another way that can be done is by looking at either their *first four years* (as each played four years – or more) or, perhaps more specifically, *from ages twenty-five to twenty-eight* (as each also played during that span in perhaps their "physical prime"). This at least removes any advantages that age would have on their performance. In this particular instance, there are other variables that come into play, starting with the fact that Bo Jackson never played an entire single football season due to his commitment on the baseball field. Did less football-related wear and tear on his body leave him stronger for when he did enter a game, where he often shared carries with Hall of Famer Marcus Allen, or did the cross training between two sports weigh on him even more, as he couldn't fully dedicated his training hours to being a running back, making his yards per carry figures even more impressive? Stretching this idea of "similar time periods" to poker, it would be much easier to compare the first twenty years of Johnny Moss's career to Phil Ivey's, but there are still so many additional variables that go into that, as the games were so different during both of their early years. If on the other hand we want to include as part of Johnny Moss's greatness the fact that he was cashing and winning World Series Of Poker events at unprecedented ages, and sticking with the point that "over time" is a valuable piece to this debate, someone like a Johnny Moss or Doyle Brunson should get extra "points" for competing against the top competitors of their time for such a long period of time.

Another distinction that will need to be made in any arena is comparing different players to players *of their time* versus comparing players against players *of different time periods*. It seems obvious but worth stating the point that the greatest of anything would emerge victorious/superior over other top competitors *of their time.* Jumping again to another sport, judging the greatest players in basketball is a bit more complex than picking just the best scorer, passer, or rebounder. Like poker, "greatest" in basketball suggests more than just being good at one aspect of the game, with some consideration given to different offensive *and* defensive demonstration as well as a variable found in all team sports, their overall contribution to the team's success. A lot of emphasis on the greatness of individuals in team sports is given to winners. While it is clear that winning teams are made up of individuals that collectively perform better than other groups of individuals, I believe it a bit unfair to put an overabundance of emphasis on the winning part. In the NBA alone, no one is placing Sam Jones, Tom Heinsohn, K.C. Jones and Tom Sanders in their Top Five NBA Players of All Time list despite them being second and tied for third place in the amount of Championship Rings each one holds. That said, winning should be given some weight to the Greatest Of All Time argument as surely some players do contribute more greatly to the overall success of the team, driving that team to emerge the last one standing at the end of the season.

Staying in the NBA, I believe a fairer way to tease out whether or not any player emerged victorious/superior over other top competitors *of their time* is to look at the number of Most Valuable Player awards each has achieved. Most Valuable Player awards, vague as their titles might suggest, hint at measuring some all-around level of greatness. While the award itself is subjective and always debatable and may not be the best measurement tool, but given it has been around for a while and spans multiple generations, let's see what it tells us. Since each is presented in the context of other players also eligible for the award, we can assume that it is at least a somewhat fair comparison of greatness of one player relative to others of their time. In the NBA, there are three Most Valuable

Player awards given each year; one for the regular season, one for the All Star Game and one for the Finals. Readers might or might not find this surprising but when all three are added up, the two players that emerge as "the greatest" are those that are commonly given the subjective title anyway, with Michael Jordan winning fourteen (five in the regular season, three in the All Star Game and six in the Finals) and LeBron James winning eleven (four in the regular season, three in the All Star Game and four in the Finals). One can argue that the All Star Game MVP isn't a great judge of greatness, given the game is not seen as highly competitive but more one for entertainment value. While that is definitely true, surely an individual's greatness is still being demonstrated, as they are playing the game relative to other individuals in the same type of venue. As a "validation" of this MVP methodology, the next two finishers are also those that many would put on their Mount Rushmore of NBA Players, with Kareem Abdul Jabbar netting eight MVPs (six in the regular season, none in the All Star Game and two in the Finals) and Magic Johnson also netting eight (three in the regular season, two in the All Star Game and three in the Finals). Shaquille O'Neill and Kobe Bryant tie for the fifth spot with seven MVPs (with the NBA All Star Game MVP Award now named after Bryant) and four players round out the top ten with six (Bill Russell, Wilt Chamberlain, Larry Bird and Tim Duncan). While some argument could be made about these awards, specifically for players like Russell and Chamberlain for playing in a time where not all the MVPs were presented (with it likely that Russell specifically would have won a few more Finals MVPs if the award was given during his Championship years) or even that it leaves out other popular nominees for greatest player (like Oscar Robertson, Elgin Baylor or Jerry West), the overall concept of measuring players by some subjective award like an MVP seems somewhat valid given that the NBA MVP "total list" mirrors who many think are the top players of all-time. The fact that the Greatest Of All Time sits atop the list, with 27% more MVP's than the runner up says something.

While the line of thinking of leveraging a "greatest" system (like the Most Valuable Player award) and simply adding them up across time periods makes some sense, it raises at least one question. What if the players of the past were simply just awful relative to players of today? An argument could be made that the best of previous eras wouldn't stand a chance competing against the best of today. I would agree that this is often most definitely true and warrants some more clarification on what we're actually trying to measure.

This leads to a deeper distinction, where an important difference between "Greatest" and "Best" is made. Throughout history, mankind has been making improvements on innovations of the past. The invention of the wheel evolved to the wagon, which evolved to the Model T which evolved to the Aston Martins that

PokerStars used to give away in their tournament series. Isaac Newton supposedly said that if he had seen further, it was by standing on the shoulder of giants. David Thompson provided the shoulders for a young Michael Jordan to stand upon and look up to, to which LeBron James and every other person who "wanted to Be Like Mike" tried to build upon, to see how much further they could take excellence. My brother is an electrician and a pretty great one at that. When my local casino needs electrical work, they call him. That said, and he concurs, that when it comes to electricity, he's no Benjamin Franklin, Thomas Edison, or Nikola Tesla, yet Foxwoods Resort Casino in Ledyard, Connecticut, would clearly hire him over them (if given the choice) given his familiarity not only with all of that learning from the past, but with all the modern tools and strategies that came after them. Is my brother a "better" electrician by today's standards than Franklin? Undoubtedly yes. For argument's sake, let's say my brother is the best electrician in the world today. With that, he is "better" than everyone else today. That would make him the "best." But is he "great"? Googling these two definitions gives us a clear clue and distinction that is going to be useful in our framework. Google's first definition of "great" includes "of an extent, amount, or intensity considerably above the normal or average." "Best" includes "of the most excellent, effective, or desirable type or quality." So, "best" notes some level of superiority, but that level can be miniscule. "Greatest" seems to hint that the difference is "considerable," which I think is an important distinction. For the record, the framework in this chapter is attempting to measure the Greatest Of All Time and not the Best of All Time. To be the best, one needs to be better than everyone else, though to be the greatest, one needs to display an even stronger superiority over everyone else currently participating in that arena, with that superiority greater than the superiority of others in different eras. If my brother is better than other electricians of today, it probably isn't by as wide a margin as Franklin's ideas were versus other "electricians" of the late 1700's. So, given that the future "player" has an inherent advantage versus previous players given the historical learnings that the modern player possesses, it seems more fair to conclude that some sort of "gap analysis" has to be included in the "Greatest" argument.

Major League Baseball seems to have a good statistic for this gap, which is called Wins Above Replacement. While the math behind the statistic is beyond the scope of this book, MLB.com defines the statistic as one that "measures a player's value in all facets of the game by deciphering how many more wins he's worth than a replacement-level player at his same position." This statistic seems to take into account not only how good a player is today relative to other players today but ever since statistics were kept. Since this statistic can be somewhat fairly reproduced for players of past eras, looking at it could be a somewhat fair comparison to that gap between the best players of today relative to the field versus the gap of players of the past to their field. The "greatest" of these players would have the largest gaps / Wins Above Replacement.

Much like the Most Valuable Player summary for the National Basketball Association, looking at the top Wins Above Replacement makes a lot of intuitive sense in that the top players who emerge are the household names of the sport. If we focus our attention to just hitters (as opposed to pitchers, who, on average, have more of an impact on their team's likelihood of a win given the larger percentage of the game with the ball in their hands/control), the All-Time Wins Above Replacement list starts with the player generally considered the Greatest Of All Time, Babe Ruth, followed by Barry Bonds, Willie Mays, Ty Cobb, and Hank Aaron. If we move to Average Wins Above Replacement per Season (to eliminate the positive/additive effect that a long career would have over a short one), it would be tough to argue that the greatest outfield that could be assembled would be one of Babe Ruth in Right Field, Mike Trout in Center Field, and Ted Williams in Left Field. While Wins Above Replacement doesn't tackle the impact of performance enhancing drugs, the exclusion of black players until 1947, the impact of going away to war (the real sort of war, not WAR...), the concept of looking at the gaps between players seems a valuable tool when comparing players of different times.

We're getting closer. We have some concept of what "all time" means in combining a long period of time, "best years" and/or "during the same age." We have some measures of greatness, whether subjective MVP ratings and/or statistical WARs. We've also made a distinction between "greatest" and "best." Is the greatest player of all time the one who held the biggest gap in superior achievement for the longest time?

If we buy into this framework so far, there are still a few more debatable points we'll want to address. What if a player meets the criteria of crushing the competition, though the competition of that time really isn't that great? As a graduate of the University of Connecticut in 1998, I saw some of this first-hand. The 1995 UConn Women's Basketball Team went 35-0 in NCAA play, winning the National Championship. It was definitely a reason to celebrate on campus, as it was the team's first championship, and it was versus (at the time) the best program for women's college basketball, the University of Tennessee, coached under Hall of Famer Pat Summitt. Pat Summitt and Tennessee dominated college basketball, though I don't think it sexist to admit that women's college basketball was still in its relative infancy during many of those years prior to 1995. There were definitely great (and future Hall of Fame) players who played prior to 1995, who could have competed with the best of the players in any era, but as a whole, with few female basketball role models to look up to, the game was not as evolved as it was today. With UConn dominating in the following decades, the competition was clearly getting better, but for a young girl watching the UConn team win in 1995 and the start of the Women's National Basketball Association formation the following year, it would still be a while before she would have multiple female role models. Even the 1995 team's best player, Rebecca Lobo, sported uniform number fifty out of admiration of her childhood hero, the male player David Robinson. All of this noted, despite the gap between UConn and the rest of the league, the gap has to be taken with some subjective understanding that despite the years that women started playing in NCAA games, the competition was still in its infancy.

"The early years" of an endeavour have a few strikes against it. One is indeed that the competition can't be as fierce, so the relative greatness, as large as it might be, has to be taken with some subjectivity. The other is of course that as time progresses, fewer first-hand stories of that greatness remain. In the sport of baseball, performance of both hitters and pitchers are separated into the "pre-modern" and "modern eras." In part due to the game changing around 1920 due to the change in how filthy balls were taken from play after Ray Chapman was killed by a pitch, statistics began to change. While fewer hitters had batting averages over .400, when they did hit the ball, they went further. Pitchers' Earned Run Averages went up, and given some of the burnout observed in the late eighteen hundreds, less innings were pitched by each hurler. While there were still clearly players who excelled in the early years of the game, many of them are often dismissed today when considering the all-time greats of the game. Few would say that Tim Keefe was a better (or greater) pitcher than Pedro Martinez (though check out both of their statistics if you want to see some insanely great numbers), though with no footage of Keefe and very few stories about him, his relative greatness versus others in his era is often overlooked.

Just one more sport before we get back to poker, as it brings an interesting perspective. Who was the greater runner, or specifically sprinter, Jesse

Owens or Usain Bolt? Bolt clearly has the fastest times to go along with the best training and nutrition. I'll hypothesize that the gap between him and second-place runners was also greater than Owens', as footage of his races often show him way out in front of others. Is there a way to remove the impact of Bolt's better sneakers and the fact that he ran on a surface clearly designed for speed – as opposed to the more energy-absorbent grounds that Owens ran? Sports Science writer David Epstein notes that one biomechanical analysis of the speed of Owens' joints shows that had he been running on the same surface as Bolt, he would have been within one stride. I think this proves a reminder that there are a lot of variables to consider when comparing players of different eras. In the case of running, it goes beyond just their clocked times, but in different ways of measuring greatness.

One thing is clear, in that we at least have to have some agreement about what the game is. Earlier we started defining "poker player" as one who plays all types of poker (different games, types, formats, etc.). As per the storyline in this book, the game of poker (in some strict sense of what the game of poker is) can be solved by a computer. Many of today's best players, leveraging computer simulations of Game Theory Optimal play, can get pretty close to ideal play if they study computer outputs. If we agree that this is ideal play, then players of the past would be no match for today's players, correct? Phil Galfond appears to be a great modern poker player; he plays multiple games, does well live and online, and performs well in cash games and tournaments. If he put out a "Galfond Challenge" to Johnny Moss to play twenty five thousand hands of No Limit Texas Hold Em, most believe that Phil would win. So does that make him a "better" poker player? I think the answer to that is yes, given today's game.

Here's a fun part though. Going back to our definition of "poker," I purposely left out one element until now. While the earlier definition attempted to describe the game of poker in terms of *ways* (like online, live, tournament, cash) and variants (No Limit Texas Hold Em, Pot Limit Omaha High Low Eight or Better, or Deuce to Seven Triple Draw), I omitted until now a different definition of "poker game" that fits best here, which might be equally important. Outside the ways and variants of the game, an actual "poker game" meant something very different in the early and middle of the twentieth century versus today. To demonstrate this simply, let's put Phil Galfond in one of Johnny Moss's games on the Texas Circuit. Is Phil Galfond going to perform as well as he would in 2020 sitting in a comfortable gaming chair in air-conditioned casino being served food and drinks that are freely given with his tournament entry fee, with security guards within a whistle away *versus* a "poker game" where he's asked to carry an armed weapon (that he is expecting to have to use at some point), keep a watchful eye not only for his opponents poker tendencies, but also cheaters in the walls/ceilings, all types of cheating opportunities with the dealers and marked cards, all with the fear that even if he does keep his wits to play great poker, that making it out of the room alive to "recognize" his winnings may be the biggest challenge? In addition, one can assume that for the most part, Johnny Moss was playing with his own money, whereas many of today's players are staked to play, given their buy-ins by an investor who expects a return on that investment, where the players themselves may only "own" 8% of their buy-in and profits. A "poker game" to Johnny Moss wasn't a 2020 poker game during most of his career.

Now let's solely focus on how we are to start making a case for the greatest poker player (and players, for our Mount Rushmore). Starting with this last point, Johnny Moss was clearly proficient in all types of poker games available to him. In his early days in the Wild West of the Texas Circuit cash games, he was clearly one of the best or the best poker player around. He was able to win at the all different variants of poker and still make it out alive. Benny Binion called *him* when he needed a high stakes player to play against Nick Dandolos. Doyle Brunson named *him* as potentially his only mentor / role model in the game. If there was an MVP to be awarded from his twenty-first birthday in 1928 until 1969, a case could be made that Moss would have won all forty-one of them. Starting in 1970, when more formal "awards" were given out (in the form of World Series of Poker wins), Moss set the record for the decade with seven. For reference, only one other player has earned seven in one decade (Phil Ivey in the 2000's), with Stu Ungar earning the most in the 1980's (four), Phil Hellmuth the 1990's (five) and Michael Mizrachi in the 2010's (five). After fifty years of World Series of Poker play, where he only played in the early years, his nine bracelets still rank fifth all-time, with only Phil Hellmuth (with fifteen), Doyle Brunson (ten), Johnny Chan (ten) and Phil Ivey (ten) ahead of him. As a reminder, all of World Series of Poker wins (and other cashes) came after his sixty second birthday.

While online poker wasn't available during Moss's playing days, he clearly excelled at tournament play, though cash games seemed to be how he made his living in his early years. Even in his later years in Las Vegas, he was found playing in the largest cash games there / in the world.

To critique his early career, one could say that the players in those early cash games weren't great poker players (which is likely true) and that the World Series of Poker fields he competed against were smaller than the modern ones (also true). To the argument of how we're measuring greatness, though, the gap between him and others was clearly huge. Surely millionaires in the oil business had some intelligence and desire to learn the games that they hosted, though Moss outperformed them. Early tournament players were among the best in the world, though he rose above them more times than they did him. His career also bridged the gap between the games of the early Texas Circuit and the modern game. Could Johnny Moss compete today? That question raises others. Are we bringing Johnny Moss back from the dead with the poker knowledge at the time of his death (1995) to battle players with knowledge from the latest twenty five years, or does Moss have that knowledge too? Again, if we sit Johnny Moss from 1970 into a game with Phil Galfond in 2020, my money is on Galfond taking an early lead. While never having access to (good) poker books or GTO calculators, Moss had the uncanny ability to know who he was playing against and find their weakness. Would he find Galfond's? When asked the question if Johnny Moss could play with the players of "today," Jack Binion gave a comical comeback that amounted to noting that the man was successful during the long span of over sixty years, with so much changing during that time; it would be laughable to think he couldn't continue to adjust. Sid Wyman, a casino owner and player who shared the inaugural induction with Johnny Moss into poker's Hall of Fame, once noted that Johnny had no weakness. It seems a tougher argument to not name Johnny Moss as the Greatest Poker Player of All Time than to give him the title.

Using the same framework of thinking, let's attempt to round out the Mount Rushmore of greatness in this game. Doyle Brunson's career seemed to mirror Moss's in that he competed and won at the early types of cash games held throughout the country. When tournament poker became popular, he became on one of its early faces, winning ten World Series of Poker bracelets and one World Poker Tour title, along with numerous final tables and cashes. Like Moss, he continues to play in is advanced years, still in the biggest games. And like Moss, despite No Limit Texas Hold Em his best game, he played all the games well. I couldn't find record of his online play, though he did have a poker playing site named after him. It doesn't take being one of the greatest to write a book (with that jab at myself intended) though he did write one of the most popular training books in the history of the game.

The gap between him and others seemed great for most of his career as well.

When it was time to name the room where the highest stakes games in the world were played, Bellagio executive and Hall of Famer Bobby Baldwin wanted to name it Chip's Room. Chip declined the honor, stating it would be bad for business – his own business! – to have his name on the door. It is hard to find any professional who had played with Chip Reese to not say he was either among the greatest or perhaps the greatest poker player of all time. Chip chose to stay out of the tournament scene for the most part, instead focusing his career in the biggest cash games in the world, which netted out as both a steadier and more robust source of income. I remember hearing a story that he played one online tournament with a large number of entrants and won it. His tournament career was highlighted in 2006, when he competed in the inaugural $50,000 H.O.R.S.E. tournament, which included a mix of variants. It was the biggest buy-in tournament at the time and meant to determine the best player, as unlike No Limit Texas Hold Em, where one lucky card could change fortunes, these five different Limit variants would require slow and steady great play to determine a winner that was deserved of an all-around poker championship. After several days of live play, one of the toughest final tables of all-time and one of the longest heads-up battles of all-time, Chip emerged the winner. That tournament has been renamed the Player's Championship and the award for winning has been renamed the Chip Reese Memorial Trophy. Chip's Las Vegas career started during the years when Johnny Moss was still playing in the big games and they both clashed several times, notably once in one of Chip's earliest hands in Las Vegas. Against three future Hall of Famer's, Chip scooped a twenty-nine thousand dollar hand in Seven Card Stud Hi Low Eight or Better with the Ace to Five Straight Flush versus the Ace High flushes of Johnny Moss and Puggy Pearson and the Full House of Doyle Brunson.

Even Johnny Moss's biography notes that "many professionals mark him to be perhaps the man who will follow in Johnny's footsteps to become the future 'Champion of Champions.'"

When Chip Reese passed away at the sad and early age of fifty-six, the title of best all-around poker player of the day seemed to fall to Phil Ivey. He has seemed to have kept that title and now often considered the best poker player ever. A poker resume does not get much more complete than his. For cash games, he plays and wins at the highest levels, whether in Las Vegas or the latest popular place to play, Macau. In terms of tournaments, his ten World Series of Poker bracelets ties him for second place with Doyle Brunson and Johnny Chan. Despite being a stellar No Limit Texas Hold Em player, none of his bracelets are in that variant, as he clearly plays all the games well. He has final tabled several World Poker Tour events and his overall tournament winnings rank him eleventh all-time at the time of this writing, with consistently high cashes contributing to that total versus just a few big scores. He is said to have won millions in the online games. Like Doyle Brunson, his MasterClass and now defunct Ivey League training site have tried to teach the game to others. Like Johnny Moss, he had his own "Nick 'The Greek'" highlight, when he took part in the Big Game against billionaire banker Andy Beal, winning over sixteen million dollars after their heads-up Limit match. The record does not show that Andy Beal uttered the phrase "Mister Ivey, I have to let you go."

Like all the great players, all four on my Mount Rushmore not only seemed to win more than most when they sat down at whatever games were being spread, but also exhibited the other characteristics of great players. They seemed to be aware of their surroundings and knew how to play against every single player at their table. Perhaps the one trait that separates these players from other greats, such as Stu Ungar and Phil Hellmuth, are their ability to stay away from that dreaded condition known as "tilt," which robs many unfortunate players of playing their A-Game, especially when they're losing or have run into bad luck. Like the traditional Buddhist monks, they seem to be/play in the moment, not let their environment impact them in a negative manner, and make the best decisions possible. They were all respected by their contemporaries and I would wager any amount that they will continue to be looked upon as among the greatest to have ever played their game, regardless of the framework used to measure their excellence versus all others.

Conclusion and Acknowledgements

To paraphrase a famous Full Tilt commercial featuring Phil Ivey, where he notes that he is "kind of" *just playing the same game we are*, I asked myself what kind of book this was. Is it a poker book? Kind of. Is it a book about artificial intelligence? Kind of. Is it a book about human intelligence and creative thinking? Kind of. Is it a book about the desire to be great or the obsession with an endeavor, that potentially has the chance to overshadow other important aspects of your life? Kind of. Is it a book that includes many lessons, some subtle and some not, that I'd like to pass on to my kids? Yes, including the one to not get started in poker. Is there a lot of good that can come from learning poker? Wholeheartedly yes. Can you be a good person while still wanting to take others' money? I think so. Are there other ways to achieve greatness while staying away from an activity that also has more than its fair share of negative elements? I'd bet yes.

The best at any "game" often have deficits elsewhere. Ty Cobb and Michael Jordan were sickly competitive. Tiger Woods was unfaithful. Babe Ruth ate too much. Warren Buffett admits to not making his family enough of a priority. Poker has its fair share of greatness clouded in negativity. Stu Ungar drugged out. Phil Ivey, well, kind of walked out of a casino with more money than they thought he should, despite later settling out of court for the disputed funds. Johnny Moss didn't seem great with handling money or family, and who really knows if he ever cheated at the game or not. So what is the lesson? Greatness comes with sacrifices, though sometimes that can be overcome. Jackie Robinson, who noted that "a life is not important except in the impact it has on other lives" made a difference. Bruce Lee and Kareem Abdul Jabbar were/are teachers and writers. Mohammed Ali and LeBron James aim(ed) to have social impact. Is the lesson to balance that striving for greatness with everything else needed to live an all-around good life? Or is the quest for greatness inherent in some, consuming the individual and overshadowing everything, making at least its quest and the negative side effects often noted unavoidable?

I hope a balance is possible and that is what I want my children to take away from this book. Having trained in the martial arts for almost thirty years, I have a competition career that the Grand Master of my art has noted includes "a tournament resume that a lot of people would envy." Since slowing down in the martial arts, I now find myself near the top of the leaderboards in the poker league we founded over ten years ago. I like to think I've balanced my competitive drive toward accomplishments while still being a good son, brother, husband, father, friend, along with doing a good job at my full-time profession. Maybe I have, maybe I haven't. Though who is going to write that story? Likely no one, and that's fine. In the meantime all we can do is do our best, striving for excellence in the areas that are importance to us.

This book doesn't get done without the recent and ongoing support and guidance from many others. To my brother Rich Chiaramonte and friend Dan Burns, thanks for the dialogue on the GOAT. Kevin Botte, I think you owe me two pennies from one of our early games in 1993. To the BASES team in New Jersey that started playing with me for more than a dollar as well as the introduction to internet poker, especially Jon Gordon, Jim McGarr, Kelly Reynolds and Tom Miskulin, thank you. To the Nielsen team in England, too many to list, but especially Sean Tunning and Rob Hallworth, who got me into the local game and have stayed in touch, thank you for all the invites to the £5 tournaments that kept my interest in the game while away from the United States. Both before, during and after my relocation to England I always had Brandon and Chris Ferraro to play with and talk poker; thank you brothers. Phil Herr, thank you for teaching me the value of storytelling. To the Millward Brown group, which transformed into the Easton Series of Poker, and again too many to list, thank you, especially Frank Chipman, Chris Thomas, Jason Mumbach, Dan Johnson, Chris Barcello, Eric Grisier, Charles Voss, and Paul Malafronte for the competition and conversation through the last ten plus years; these games don't go on without you. And of course Adam Lee, for the partnership and leadership of the league and endless conversations about poker and life, with many during flights to Las Vegas, thank you. To the entire Loomis crew, especially Juan de Choudens for the initial invite and Joe Coldebella, Steve Micolo and Dennis Diaz, for keeping me around at the tournaments and cash games, thank you all for my new poker home away from home. Nathan Gamble, I hardly know you, but thank you for taking the time to help take my Pot Limit Omaha High Low Eight or Better game to the next level. To my "accountability group" of Christine Prentice and Alexis Stevens, thanks for the continued motivation to achieve a goal. I don't get much done without the weekday support of Laura Burke, whose friendship and ear I value more than most over the last twenty-five years plus, thank you. My parents may not have started out being the biggest poker fans in the world but every night I rest assured that there does not exist a stronger love and support for me than from them, to which I am eternally thankful. My wife Suzanne and boys, Eddie and Leo, thanks for allowing me some time to write and allowing me to share some of the joys of writing my first book. Boys, I hope this book inspires your own greatness while you maintain the kindness and empathy that your mom and I taught you. You are both already the Greatest Of All Time in my book and your stories have just begun.

Collection of Johnny Moss Poker Chips

- Alvarez, A. *The Biggest Game in Town*. San Francisco, CA, Chronicle Books, 1983.

- Bradshaw, Jon. *Fast Company, How Six Master Gamblers Defy the Odds – and Always Win*. New York, NY, Vintage Departures, Vintage Books, Random House, 1975.

- Brunson, Doyle. *According to Doyle / Poker Wisdom of a Champion, Powerful Winning Advice and Fascinating Anecdotes From Poker's Greatest Player*. New York, NY, Cardoza Publishing, 1984.

- Brunson, Doyle. *How I Made Over $1,000,000 Playing Poker / Super/System, A Course in Power Poker*. Las Vegas, NV, B & G Publishing, Co., Inc., 1978.

- Brunson, Doyle. *My 50 Most Memorable Hands*. New York, NY, Cardoza Publishing, 2007.

- Brunson, Doyle. *The Godfather of Poker, An Autobiography*. New York, NY, Cardoza Publishing, 2007.

- Carnegie Mellon University. "AI beats professionals in six-player poker." *Science Daily*, 11 July 2019,

https://www.sciencedaily.com/releases/
2019/07/190711141343.htm

- Chaffin, Sean. "Artificial Intelligence Tops Humans in Poker Battle – What's the Big Deal?" *Pokernews*, 6 February 2017, https://www.pokernews.com/news/2017/02/artificial-intelligence-tops-humans-in-poker-battle-27044.htm

- Craig, Michael. *The Professor, The Banker, and The Suicide King.* New York, NY, Grand Central Publishing, 2006.

- Dalla, Nolan. "The Ecstasy of Gold." *NolanDalla.com.* 6 July 2013, https://www.nolandalla.com/ecstasy-gold/

- Greenstein, Barry. *Ace on the River, An Advanced Poker Guide.* Fort Collins, CO, Last Knight Publishing Company, 2005.

- Hale, "Oklahoma Johnny." *The Life and Times of a Gentleman Gambler.* Las Vegas, NV, Poker Plus Publications, 1999.

- http://m.mlb.com/glossary/advanced-stats/wins-above-replacement#
  :~:text=Definition,fill%2Din%20free%20agent)

- http://www.thehypertexts.com/Baseball%20Leaders%20in%20WAR%20per%20162%20game%20season.htm
- https://en.wikipedia.org/wiki/1994%E2%80%9395_Connecticut_Huskies_women%27s_basketball_team
- https://en.wikipedia.org/wiki/Henry_Orenstein
- https://en.wikipedia.org/wiki/Johnny_Moss
- https://en.wikipedia.org/wiki/NBA_All-Star_Game_Kobe_Bryant_Most_Valuable_Player_Award
- https://en.wikipedia.org/wiki/NBA_Finals_Most_Valuable_Player_Award
- https://en.wikipedia.org/wiki/NBA_Most_Valuable_Player_Award
- https://en.wikipedia.org/wiki/Ray_Chapman
- https://en.wikipedia.org/wiki/Sahara_Las_Vegas
- https://en.wikipedia.org/wiki/Watson_(computer)
- https://en.wikipedia.org/wiki/World_Series_of_Poker_bracelet
- https://pokerdb.thehendonmob.com/
- https://www.baseball-reference.com/leaders/WAR_career.shtml
- https://www.conjelco.com/hof95/17-Dec-hof.html
- https://www.doylebrunson.com/media/interviews/

- https://www.legacy.com/obituaries/oaoa/obituary.aspx?n=eleoweese-moss-elder&pid=164950711&fhid=14321

- https://www.pro-football-reference.com/players/B/BrowJi00.htm

- https://www.pro-football-reference.com/players/J/JackBo00.htm

- https://www.pro-football-reference.com/players/S/SandBa00.htm

- https://www.wsop.com/

- Hughes, Johnny. "When the Most Famous Gambler in the World was a Shill." *Bluff Europe*, 1 April 2010, http://www.bluffeurope.com/poker-news/en/editorial/When-the-Most-Famous-Gambler-in-the-World-was-a-Shill_7110.aspx

- Jenkins, Don. *Poker's Finest, Champion of Champions, A Portrait of the Greatest Poker Player of Our Time.* USA, Johnny Moss, 1981.

- Kasparov, Garry. *Deep Thinking: Where Machine Intelligence Ends and Human Creativity Begins.* New York, NY, PublicAffairs, 2017.

- Keith The Dealer. Conversation. Binion's Gambling Hall, Las Vegas, NV, 2018.

- Konic, Michael. "The Grand Old Man of Poker." *Cigar Aficionado*, Winter 1995/96, pp. 206-211.

- Lee, Bruce. *Tao of Jeet Kune Do*. Santa Clarita, CA, Ohara Publications, 1975.

- Lucchesi, Ryan. "WSOP: History -- 1970 Recap." *Cardplayer*, 4 June 2008, https://www.cardplayer.com/poker-news/4323-wsop-history-1970-recap.

- Lucchesi, Ryan. "WSOP: History -- 1971 Recap." *Cardplayer*, 5 June 2008, https://www.cardplayer.com/poker-news/4335-wsop-history-1971-recap.

- Lucchesi, Ryan. "WSOP: History -- 1972 Recap." *Cardplayer*, 6 June 2008, https://www.cardplayer.com/poker-news/4345-wsop-history-1972-recap.

- Lucchesi, Ryan. "WSOP: History -- 1973 Recap." *Cardplayer*, 7 June 2008, https://www.cardplayer.com/poker-news/4352-wsop-history-1973-recap.

- Lucchesi, Ryan. "WSOP: History -- 1974 Recap." *Cardplayer*, 8 June 2008, https://www.cardplayer.com/poker-news/4354-wsop-history-1974-recap.

- Mallenbaum, Carly. "Usain Bolt vs. Jesse Owens: Here's the tale of the tape." *USA Today*, 18 February 2016, https://www.usatoday.com/story/life/entertainthis/2016/02/18/lets-all-appreciate-how-fast-jesse-owens/80523426/

- McManus, James. *Cowboys Full, The Story of Poker*. New York, NY, Farrar, Straus and Giroux, 2009.

- *Paul Bunyan*. Directed by Les Clark, Walt Disney, 1958.

- Rinkema, Remko. "Dealing to Doyle Brunson & Fired By Johnny Moss, David Heyden Has Seen It All." *Poker Central*, 4 July 2019, https://www.pokercentral.com/articles/dealing-doyle-brunson-fired-johnny-moss-david-heyden-seen/.

- Shrake, Edwin. "The World's Best Poker Player." *Sports Illustrated*, 25 January, 1971, pp. 56-66.

- Schmich, Mary. "Advice, like youth, probably just wasted on the young." *Chicago Tribune*, 1 June 1997, https://www.chicagotribune.com/ columns/chi-schmich-sunscreen-column-column.html.

- *The Cincinnati Kid.* Directed by Norman Jewison, Metro-Goldwyn-Mayer, 1965.

Additional Pages About Johnny Moss

- http://archive.bluff.com/magazine/remembering-johnny-moss-9000/
- http://www.virtualubbock.com/stoJHughes_Moss.html
- https://analyzepoker.com/blog/johnny-moss-the-poker-legend/
- https://lasvegassun.com/news/1996/apr/22/binion-chip-immortalizes-poker-player/
- https://play.google.com/store/books/details?id=fCMG5u vYEm8C&gl=us&hl=en-US&source=productsearch&utm_source=HA_Desktop_US &utm_medium=SEM&utm_campaign=PLA&pcampaignid= MKTAD0930BO1&gclid=EAIaIQobChMIuYDvktj_6gIVo9Sz Ch35YQwJEAQYBCABEgJpovD_BwE&gclsrc=aw.ds
- https://www.gamblinggurus.com/gambling-legends/johnny-moss/
- https://www.lasvegasadvisor.com/gambling-with-an-edge/the-cheating-game/

- https://www.oaoa.com/news/article_a4c90e09-60a5-5eb7-a9a3-f94ba9cbaf52.html
- https://www.pokerlistings.com/13-hard-to-believe-stats-from-the-world-series-of-poker-93125
- https://www.texasmonthly.com/articles/the-best-gamblers-in-texas/
- https://www.youtube.com/watch?v=g9gheNWRHBc